MY
HOMEWORK
ATE MY
HOMEWORK

Other Books by Patrick Jennings

Guinea Dog
Lucky Cap
Invasion of the Dognappers

MY HOMEWORK ATE MY HOMEWORK

Patrick Jennings

EGMONT
USA
NEW YORK

For Lauren and Lex,
my homework buddies

EGMONT
We bring stories to life

First published by Egmont USA, 2013
443 Park Avenue South, Suite 806
New York, NY 10016

Copyright © Patrick Jennings, 2013
All rights reserved

3 5 7 9 8 6 4 2

www.egmontusa.com
www.patrickjennings.com

Library of Congress Cataloging-in-Publication Data

Jennings, Patrick.
My homework ate my homework / Patrick Jennings.
p. cm.
Summary: "When Zaritza is assigned to care for her class ferret Bandito over winter break, he
escapes and eats her other assignments, leaving her with an unbelievable excuse!"-- Provided by
publisher.
ISBN 978-1-60684-286-7 (hardcover) -- ISBN 978-1-60684-288-1 (electronic book) [1. Ferrets as
pets--Fiction. 2. Homework--Fiction. 3. Family life--Fiction. 4. Humorous stories.] I. Title.
PZ7.J4298715My 2013
[Fic]--dc23
2012025062

Printed in the United States of America

Contents

1. My Homework Ate My Dog

"Can I talk to you a minute, Mr. O.?" I say to the mirror. "You'd better sit down."

I make a face that shows how sorry I would be if what I was saying were true. The sunglasses holding my hair back aren't working. They make me look too glamorous, and that's not the look I'm after. I pull them off and my strawberry blonde hair tumbles down over my shoulders. This is worse. I make a mental note to stop washing my hair a few days before returning to school.

"It's about Bandito," I say and pause . . . . . . dramatically. I love dramatic pauses. They're very . . . . . . dramatic.

"You see . . . . . . I can't seem to find him. I'm sorry."

I cast my eyes downward. Casting your eyes downward is very effective, especially if you want somebody to think you feel bad about something you did. Even if you don't.

Casting them upward, by the way, is good if you want to pretend to be thinking, or trying to remember something. For example, I look up when I say, "I'm pretty sure I turned that in, Mr. O.," even though I know I didn't do the assignment. Casting your eyes sideways makes you look like you're making up an excuse, or just plain fibbing. Only do this on purpose and onstage. It's important to control sideways looks in real life. They can give you away.

Practicing eye-casting is difficult to do in a mirror, so I'm video-recording myself on my mother's cell phone.

"How did Bandito get out of his cage?" I ask rhetorically. "I don't know, Mr. O.," and shrug my shoulders up to my ears. I really look like I don't know that I left the ferret's cage door open after I fed him. Which is what happened.

Now I shift from faux-clueless to faux-suspicious. (*Faux* is French for *fake* and is pronounced *foe*, like friend or foe, and makes *fake* sound fancier.)

"I'm pretty positive my baby sister, Abalina, opened the cage door," I say, and tighten my lips, like I'm holding back anger. "That girl is always getting into my stuff."

No. I don't want to come across as blaming, especially of a baby. A baby isn't responsible for her actions. Or so my mother keeps telling me. But that's another story.

I reach up and make an erasing motion with my hand. I'm starting over.

"My baby sister, Abalina, probably opened the cage door, but she's just a baby and isn't responsible for her actions, so I'm not angry at her."

That's good. I'll keep that.

"But then something awful happened."

No, not quite right. I "erase" it.

"But then something *terrible* happened."

Better, but still no. Erase.

"But then something HORRIBLE happened!"

Yes, that's it. Now I swallow loud enough for

him to hear, flash a faux-horrified-bordering-on-sick-to-my-stomach face, pause dramatically . . . . . . then deliver my well-rehearsed punch line: "My homework ate my dog."

2. My Homework Ate My Brain

Bandito is my homework and he is hideous. Sure, he has a shiny brown-and-white fur coat, kind of like a cat's, but instead of covering an adorable purring kitty, it covers a creepy, wheezy, slithery ferret. Bandito has ratlike toes and ratlike ears, a twitching ratlike nose, and a white face with a raccoonlike black mask. He's a mustelid, which means he's cousins with stinky skunks and weasels.

Although Bandito lives in a cage way in the back corner, he stinks up every inch of my classroom. He smells like a combo of sewage and boiled cabbage. Having to smell him all day long has affected my learning. That's right: My homework has harmed my young brain.

We get extra credit points if we make notes in the Ferret Observations notebook, so lots of kids who are done with their work sit by Bandito's cage and record the mustelid's clicking, wheezing, and slithering. They must have to hold their breath while they do it. I would . . . if I ever sat there. Which I don't.

I could use extra credit points, but you can't get any unless you've finished all your work. Doesn't Mr. O. know that it's the students who don't turn in all their work who *need* extra credit? Talk about unjust.

I got pretty far behind in math—mostly because I think math is stupid and don't like doing it—and I wanted to get a passing grade on my report card, so I suggested to Mr. O. that we make a deal: I'd take Bandito for winter break and write daily notes in the Ferret Observations notebook if he would forget about the math assignments I didn't finish. This seemed just to me. Just as in the opposite of unjust, I mean.

Shockingly, Mr. O. said no deal, but he did say he'd count watching Bandito as extra credit "if and only if" I returned from the break with the ferret, the Ferret Observations notebook filled with two weeks of notes, *and* the completed math assignments. Whoa. The guy obviously doesn't understand what a break is.

I said, "That's unjust, but okay. Deal." And we shook on it.

When my mother picked me up at the end of the day and I told her I was ferret-sitting, she got all motherish on me.

"The ferret is *your* responsibility, Zaritza," she said. "You must keep the cage clean, and feed and water the ferret every day without being told, and *blah blah blahbity blah . . .*"

It was a huge mistake bringing Bandito home. He makes my room smell like sewage and boiled cabbage. I have to clean up his nasty mess every day. As a bonus I get to spend nights with a chattering, wheezing mustelid. He's so creepy that I haven't slept once during the whole vacation. Or not deeply anyway.

So when I discovered he had escaped, I didn't bother looking for him. I didn't want to find him, so why should I look? Besides, finding him would mean I'd have to catch him, which would mean

I'd have to *touch* him, which I will never do as long as I live.

He's the one who wanted out so bad. Now he's out, and he can stay out forever for all I care. If he changes his mind and wants back in, fine. I left the cage door open.

Which is how he got out in the first place. Not that I'll be telling anyone that.

Did my homework (Bandito) eat my "dog"? Maybe. I haven't checked.

I use finger quotes because Wormy isn't what I would call a real dog. Wormy isn't his real name. I named him that. His real name was Sugar, which didn't suit him at all. My father's great-aunt Veronica gave him to us when she got sick once and couldn't take care of him. Which is a decent reason, I guess, to dump a pet on your family. She could have mentioned, though, that Sugar came loaded with intestinal worms.

Then, a week later, my mother found out she (my mother, not Wormy) was expecting Abalina. That's right, both the "dog" and the baby sister were surprises. I wasn't, of course. I was planned. Wanted. Not something my parents got stuck with.

Wormy is (was?) a Maltipoo, and extremely hyper and noisy, usually at the same time. He's always freaking out about nothing and going *ARF! ARF! ARF! ARF! ARF! ARF!* in a high, annoying voice, like one of those remote-control dogs that move around with stiff legs. He's covered with kinky white fur that feels like doll's hair, and he has shiny black eyes like black marbles. I really think he isn't a dog. I think he's an evil dogdroid monster sent here by Great-Aunt Veronica to drive us all crazy.

So if Bandito did eat Wormy, the only real downside would be that I'll get in big trouble with my mother and Mr. O., which would be unjust, since the only thing I did wrong was forget to lock the cage after I refilled my homework's food dish. Yes, I fed him. Big crime. Lock me up and throw away the key. It serves me right for being thoughtful. And how does he repay my thought-fulness? By escaping and gobbling up my "dog" and getting me in trouble with my mother and my teacher. Talk about ungrateful.

Now I have to pretend I care about him, and about my revolting little "dog," too. I'll also have to lie to my teacher, and maybe frame my baby sister. I don't have a choice there. I'm certainly not going to take all the blame. That would mean having to listen to my mother talk about responsibility and consequences for the rest of my life. Abalina doesn't have any responsibilities or consequences, so what difference does it make if I pin the ferret's escape on her?

"My homework ate my dog, Mr. O.," I say again to my reflection, punching the words *homework* and *dog*. I don't finger-quote *dog* this time, because I want Mr. O. to believe that I care about Wormy, which, of course, I do not. I convey shock and horror by opening my eyes wide, then cast them downward to convey regret and grief. I add, "I couldn't feel worse about it," choking up on the word *worse*.

Good. That works.

3. My Homework Ate My Vacation

"Wormy is a Maltipoo," I say to the mirror, "and Maltipoos are tiny little dogs. Tiny enough, I imagine, that a ferret could . . ."

I let my voice trail off, then make a sick face, like I'm imagining what a ferret could do to a tiny doglike creature like Wormy. I don't actually imagine it, because the thought of it makes me gag. Hideous eating hideous.

It would serve Wormy right if the skunk-rat ate him. The "dog" and the skunk-rat ruined my vacation. Not to mention I didn't get what I wanted for Christmas, which was my ears pierced. My mother said maybe I'll be old enough next year, and I said, "You do understand that I am eleven now, right?"

Her reply? "Please don't speak that way to me."

In other words, she changed the subject. Which is just so unjust.

What did I get instead? Clothes, books, and a pink calculator. A calculator! This was from my not-great-in-the-slightest great-aunt Veronica, the one who dumped the "dog" on us. I wish my grandpa never had a sister, either.

Sisters. Who needs them?

I bet my mother put Great-Aunt Veronica up to the calculator, probably because I don't do my math. I don't need a calculator *or* math. What I need are holes in my earlobes. I've explained to my mother that an actor must be able to wear earrings. Then I had a meltdown, and my mother called me a drama queen. Which is true. I am an actor, and a queen. I take it as a compliment.

I've acted in lots of plays. I was the lead in my kindergarten's production of *The Marshmallow and the Frog.* I was the marshmallow. In first grade, I was the straw-house pig in the charming musical comedy *Little Pig! Little Pig!* I played a fairy in *A Midsummer Night's Dream,* which is Shakespeare and was performed outside. Shakespeare in the Park, they call it. I didn't have any lines, but I stole the show.

I hope to play the starring role in *Calamity Jane*, which the Laramie Traveling Children's Theater Troupe is bringing to our school in January. I've watched the movie four times and have been rehearsing the part. I feel pretty good that I'll get it.

So, yeah, I'm a drama queen. Unfortunately, I'm a drama queen with unpierced ears.

Where was I?

Oh, right. My homework ate my "dog."

"I'm very sorry that Bandito got away," I say to my reflection, "but I hope you will consider that I am grieving, too."

I pause here so he can feel bad for me, but also because Wormy has just entered my room, without permission, and is now curling up in my purple beanbag chair. The squeaking of his nails on the vinyl makes my skin crawl.

I guess my homework didn't eat my "dog" after all. Pity.

This is actually the first time Wormy has come

into my room since I brought Bandito home with me, and that's because Wormy is terrified of Bandito. This has been the one good thing about ferret-sitting: no "dog" in my room. Now that Bandito's gone, in trots Wormy the annoying little bot-hound. I just can't win.

Bandito wasn't afraid of Wormy, of course. Who would be? Mr. O. told us ferrets hiss or scream when they're scared, but Bandito didn't hiss or scream when he met Wormy. He did the "weasel war dance." He hopped around, clucking *Dook! Dook! Dook!* It sounded like he was laughing. Ferrets do the weasel war dance when they're happy, and usually what makes them happy is finding something to eat. I think that's why I got the idea that Bandito might like to eat Wormy.

But he didn't eat him.

I go back to the mirror.

"Bandito did the weasel war dance when he saw Wormy," I say. "You said ferrets do that when they're excited, and that hunters use ferrets to help them kill small animals, like rabbits and stuff. Well"—I gulp—"Wormy isn't much bigger than most rabbits."

I choke myself up and work on producing some tears. I do this by flaring my nostrils and tightening my face muscles. I feel a mist gathering behind my eyes and my tear ducts tingle. I learned in theater camp last summer that, if you want to make yourself cry, it helps to visualize something heartbreaking. So I visualize gold hoop earrings. That does the trick. I blink and a tear squirts out.

"I accept"—I sob—"full responsibility, Mr. O., for letting Bandito escape." The tear streams down my cheek, over my lip, and into my mouth. Mmmm, salty.

"The ferret escaped?" my mother shrieks from behind me.

I jump out of my skin.

4. My Homework Ate My Parka

"You scared me to death!" I say, clutching my heart. "What happened to knocking?"

My mother is standing in my doorway holding Abalina in her arms. Abby can walk. She's been doing it for quite some time now. A whole month, I think. She just doesn't want to. All she ever says is, "Uppy! Uppy!" What's the point of having legs if you don't use them?

"Zuzza!" she says.

Yeah, she talks now, too. But she still cries and screams when she wants something. I think she's pretending. She knows how to talk and walk, but she gets more attention when she doesn't.

Wormy wakes up and starts his battery-operated barking: *ARF! ARF! ARF! ARF!*

"The ferret didn't really eat Wormy, I see," my mother says.

"You heard that?"

She reaches over and swings the open cage door back and forth.

"You need to find him, Zaritza," she says.

"Why me? I didn't let him out. It was probably Abalina. She's always getting into my stuff, and you never get mad at *her*!"

"Abalina just got up from a three-hour nap," my mother says, and, on cue, Abby yawns. This is no innocent baby girl.

"Oh," I say, then turn my blame on the yapping "dog." "Shut up, Wormy! You woke the baby!"

"No, he didn't," my mother says. "He was in here with you, remember? Abalina woke up on her own."

"Why don't we have Wormy find Bandito? He's a 'dog,' so to speak."

"Because it isn't Wormy's responsibility. It's yours. You let Bandito out, and you must find him. You can't shirk your responsibilities, Zaritza. We all have them. . . ."

"Oh, really? Abalina has them? And Wormy? What are his responsibilities?"

"Abby's a baby—"

"She's *not* a baby," I cut in. "She's over a year old now. I know it's hard for you to face that your *favorite* little girl is growing up—"

"—and Wormy's a dog."

"Really? You sure about that?"

"And you are an eleven-year-old girl who agreed to take care of the class ferret."

"Fur!" Abby says.

"He's a *ferret*, Abby," I tell her, ignoring my mother. "He *has* fur, but he's a ferret. *Fair. It.*"

"Stop being disrespectful," my mother says. "Face your responsibilities, and find the ferret."

She sets her hand on her hip, pulls in her chin, and gives me the stink eye. This is her end-of-discussion move. I do it pretty well myself. I especially like using it on Abby.

"Usually, when Bandito gets out of his cage at school, he just goes back in on his own," I say, though it's not true. We usually have to trap him or coax him back in. I don't, of course. I let my classmates do it. I pretend to help when really I'm silently praying they never find him, that he got out of the building and will never be seen again.

Now, I'm not an animal hater or something. To me a lovable animal is a cat or a real dog, not some dinky yapper or some stinky weasel. That thing really *stinks*.

"We're not at school," my mother says, which is so obvious I can't help rolling my eyes. She hates when I roll them. "We're at home," she says, raising her voice, though I was hearing her just fine, "and I don't want a ferret running loose, leaving his scent and chewing things up."

"I don't want that, either, Mother! You think I want that?" I always call her "Mother." It's more dramatic than "Mom." I also call my father "Father." "Dad" is just silly.

"Wum!" Abalina says, pointing at the door.

My mother and I look at the door, but there's no one there, so we look at the bed and the bean-bag chair. No "dog." There's growling coming from somewhere. And a clucking sound.

"Fur!" Abalina says.

"For the last time, Abalina, Bandito is a *ferret*!" I say.

"Don't yell at her," Mother yells. "Go find them! Don't let them fight!"

I stare at her. "You mean get between them? I don't want to get between them. I don't want to go anywhere near either one of them."

Mother stomps her foot on the carpet, which is childish.

"Okay, okay, I'm going," I say, and hurry out of the room to search for the animals I never wanted and stop them from killing each other.

I find Wormy in the living room, *ARF-ARF-ARF*ing at my parka.

"Shut up, Wormy!" I say, but does he? No.

ARF! ARF! ARF! ARF! ARF! ARF! ARF! ARF! ARF!

That's when I see my parka move.

5. My Homework Ate My Stroopwafels

"Mother!" I scream. "He's in my coat! I can't ever wear it again!"

Bandito pokes his masked face out of one of my parka sleeves.

"Fur!" Abby says.

"He's probably after my stroopwafels," I say. "I have a full box in the pocket."

Stroopwafels are syrup-filled waffle cookies from Holland that cost a lot of money and are my very favorite treat in the world. I like to set them on a cup of hot tea and let the syrup melt. Yum.

And now the mustelid is licking them. Yuck.

"Just get him, will you, Zaritza?" Mother whines. "I'll deal with Wormy."

Wormy is snarling now. I bet he thinks he's scary. Pathetic.

"Oh, sure. You take the easy job!"

"The ferret is your respons—"

"Okay, Mother, I'll get him, I'll get him. Just *please* don't say the R-word again."

Mother snags the "dog" and locks him in the coat closet, where he whines and scratches at the door. Meanwhile, I tiptoe toward the trembling parka. I bend over slowly and quietly, then grab hold of its furry hem and pull it toward me. It slides easier than I thought it would, considering there's a mustelid in it. It's probably because the outside of the parka is made of that material that makes *whish-whish* sounds when you move your arms.

I give the parka a quick shake, but Bandito doesn't come out, so I jerk it hard and yell, "Get out of my coat, fur!"

My mother says, "Pick up the parka with him inside and take it to your room and transfer him to his cage."

"*Transfer* him? Does that mean cram the stupid weasel in, then go wash my hands with acid to get the smell off?"

"Put the parka sleeve through the cage door, then close off the other openings. He'll have to come out eventually."

It's not a bad idea. I just wish someone else would carry it out.

"Okay, here goes." I scoop up my coat and feel a hideous, muscular wriggling inside it, like I've captured a giant fish. The fish hisses. I want to scream and drop it on the floor, but I don't. Mother would just make me chase it down again. I grit my teeth, and hustle down the hallway to my room.

My mother, with Abalina in her arms, comes in behind me. "That's it. Now slip him into the cage."

"I'm going to shove the whole parka in!" I scream. I don't know why I'm screaming. Probably because I'm freaking out. "He can use it for a bed. I'm never wearing it again anyway. It stinks like ferret."

"Fur!" Abalina says.

"*Ferret*, Abby! Ferret, ferret, ferret!"

I'm glad I left the cage door open. I try to shove the parka in, but it's too puffy. Bandito panics and starts scrambling. I feel his claws through the parka.

"I can't hold him!"

Mother rushes toward me, but since she's still holding Abalina, she can't do anything.

Bandito slips out of the parka and disappears the second he hits the floor. His claws scratch at the carpet as he scurries away.

Mother starts to freak. "Where'd he go? Where'd he go? Where'd he go?"

"I don't know! I don't know! I don't know!"

Abby points under my bed. "Fur," she says.

My mother sets Abby on the bed, then she and I kneel down and peek under it. No mustelid. He must have slipped out.

"Where's the fur, Abby?" I ask.

She points a chubby finger at the door.

"He's out again," Mother groans.

"Well, why didn't you close the *door*?"

She glares at me, her face all red and wrinkly. I guess that's what happens to your face when you have a second kid at thirty-seven. My mother's a doctor. She should have known better. I have no idea why some people are never satisfied with what they have.

She mouths, *Find the ferret.*

"Okay, okay! It's always me! 'Find the ferret!' 'Pick up the ferret!' 'Transfer the ferret!'"

"Fur!" Abby says.

I whirl around to correct her again. but, with an innocent face, she says, "Uppy!"

"Can't right now, Abby," I say. "I have a fur to trap."

That's when I notice the crumbs in my parka pocket.

"My homework ate my stroopwafels!"

6. My Homework Ate . . .

We search under the couch, chairs, and tables, in the shower and tub, behind the stove and fridge. No weasel.

"Shut up, Wormy!" I yell every time I go by the coat closet. I also bang on the door with my fist.

"It's not his fault," my mother tells me. "Maybe Bandito went back to your room." Her eyes shifted side to side. This doesn't mean she's guilty. Casting your eyes sideways can also read "scared." She's afraid of the ferret.

"We already checked there and you shut the door after we left, right?" I ask.

She doesn't answer.

"You *did* shut it after we left, didn't you?"

"I don't think I did," she says, raising her shoulders.

"When are you going to learn to close doors?"

"Just be glad I haven't locked myself in the car till this thing is caught."

In my room, I say in a heavy, parent-style voice, "Close the door behind you, please."

She does.

"Thank you. Now everybody be quiet. I know this creature. He keeps me awake every night. He's never quiet. Ever. So *shhhh!*"

In the silence I hear Wormy whining in the coat closet. I hear a car door slam.

"Duh!" Abby squeals.

I hiss for her to shut up.

"Duh," she whispers.

"I know Father's home," I say to her. "Mother, don't let him in. He'll make too much noise. Stand in front of the door."

She does.

The front door slams and my father calls out, "Hello? Anyone home? The man of the house has returned! Where are my pipe and slippers? Wormy? Fetch my newspaper, boy! Well, not my newspaper boy. We don't even have a newspaper boy. Ha! Are you listening, family? Family?"

I don't have much time before he gets here. I close my eyes and listen. I hear my father's footsteps in the hall. I hear the furnace shutting off, and the warm air stops puffing out of the grate on the wall. I hear paper being crumpled. No, not crumpled. *Chewed.*

I creep toward the sound, which is coming from my rolltop desk, the one Grandpa Jack gave me. The rolltop is open slightly. Mr. O. says that ferrets can squeeze through surprisingly small openings. Hunters use them to "ferret" rabbits out of their hiding places. What is Bandito ferreting out of my desk? I do have more stroopwafels in there. . . .

"Is he in there?" my mother whispers behind me.

"Just keep Father out," I whisper back.

There's a musical knocking on the door. "Jingle Bells," I think.

"Santa's here!" my father says in a deep, jolly voice. "Ho, ho, ho!"

He turns the handle, but Mother leans hard on the door.

"Not now, Paul," she whispers through the keyhole. "Keep quiet for a minute, please."

"Okay," he whispers. "Girl stuff, eh? I'll leave you to it."

I flash my mother a thumbs-up, then move closer to the desk. I peek through the crack. Should I slam the rolltop shut, trapping him inside? I don't really want him trapped in my desk. He's already eating something. And then there's the opposite end of that: I don't want to find ferret droppings in there.

The other option is to pull open the rolltop, but that would mean I'd have to grab the squirming, hissing mustelid and wrestle him into his cage. I don't want to do that.

I don't see another way, unfortunately. Sometimes you just have to man up and get 'er done. Am I right?

No, that's just dialogue from some stupid action movie I saw. I'm no action hero.

But . . . I am an actor, just like the guy who read that line. I can play the part. I can act like I'm brave. Acting is what I do best.

"Okay," I say to my mother, my eyes all squinty

like a movie cowboy. "Keep the child back. I'm going in."

I stand up straight and take a fearless step toward my desk. I hook my fingers under the rolltop and fling it open. The ferret is in there, cowering under the little cubbies. He's feasting on one of my notebooks. It's my *math* notebook.

"Oh, no!" I shriek in horror. "My homework ate my . . . . . ."

(Did I mention I love dramatic pauses?)

7. . . . My Homework!

"My homework ate my homework!" I exclaim.

"Don't yell! Get it! Grab him!"

"Here now, what's all the screaming about?" my father says in a deep voice. "Everything all right in there? Back away from the door. I'm going to break it down."

He doesn't mean it. My father's an actor, too. A drama king.

"Let him in," I say to my mother. "We'll let the big, strong man catch the wild beast."

Mother opens the door wide enough for Father to slip inside. He's wearing casual clothes, not school clothes, since it's vacation. He's got on blue jeans and his T-shirt that says MY BIKE TIRE IS ♭ on the front and I MUST HAVE RUN OVER SOMETHING ♯ on the back. When there's school he wears a short-sleeve, button-up shirt, usually in a pastel color, with a tie. His ties usually have a musical theme, like notes, or clefs, or piano keys. Father studied theater in college and has acted in a lot of plays, a few of them in Seattle, in fact, but he's also a singer and a musical genius. He's taught choir at the high school since I started first grade.

"Father, Father!" I say with faux dread. "Please save your womenfolk from this savage beast!" I lay the back of my hand on my forehead, as if I'm about to faint.

He swoops into the room and steps between me and the ferret. "Stand back, fair lass. This is the job for ...... a choir director!"

I get my love for dramatic pauses from him.

"The beast has devoured all of my hard labor, kind sir," I say, and sob into my sleeve.

"Fie on the fiend! Hard labor is what he'll soon know, for I shall dispatch the vile badger to the nearest penitentiary."

"Duh!" Abalina squeals.

"The child is cute, but please remove it from this perilous place," Father says to Mother. "Perhaps you might go yonder and release the hounds. Or hound, as the case may be. It is howling like a banshee."

Mother groans, "Just get the badger back in its cage, Paul," and carries Abby out.

"And close the door behind you this time!" I say.

She does.

"Let's snag that beast!" Father says.

"Pray, will not the creature harm you?" I clasp my hands together tightly, and pretend to bite a knuckle. This would work better if I were wearing dainty white gloves, but you have to work with what you have. We actors call this "improvising," or, for short, "improv."

"It will surely do its best, but I am not wholly inexperienced in these matters, my dear. Why, once, when I was no bigger than you, I tangled with a rampaging snow leopard—"

"Forgive the interruption, sir, but maybe we can save your tales of heroism for a later time?"

He pretends to be embarrassed. "No, forgive *me*, miss! You are absolutely right!"

He inches toward the desk, crouched like a wrestler. Bandito quits hissing and starts making happy clucking sounds. He likes my father. Maybe it's because Father likes him. Father likes everyone. Even mustelids. Before you know it, Bandito is climbing Father's arm to his shoulder and starts nuzzling his neck. It's almost cute. Almost.

"The savage beast has been tamed!" Father proclaims. "Say, that tickles, savage beast." He faux-giggles.

"Please put him back in his cage," I say. "I want to see how much damage he did to my homework. He already ate my stroopwafels."

"The scoundrel," Father says as he locks Bandito up. "We'll add theft to the charges of attempted escape and wanton destruction of property."

"Just look at my homework! Ruined! All that hard work gone to waste!"

Actually, I'd barely started it. I have eight math assignments to make up, but every time I think about starting them, I stop breathing. My body knows it's unfair to ask it to do math on vacation. One time I did stick it out and got through two problems before collapsing onto the floor, gasping for air. And now those problems are in shreds!

I slam the rolltop shut, almost on my father's fingers.

"Sorry," I say. "I just . . . . . . can't bear to look at it!"

"I understand, cupcake."

"I was almost *finished*." I start tightening my face muscles, flattening my nose, visualizing huge gold hoop earrings.

"I guess you'll have to redo them then." He gives me a gentle squeeze. "Don't worry. I'll help you."

"*Redo* them?" I twist away from him, and tears actually fly from my eyes. Excellent! "I can't possibly *redo* them. School starts back up on *Tuesday*. Tuesday! That's only"—I count on my fingers—"only three days! And I have to take care of the beast. And record his behavior. I don't have *time*. I just don't have t-t-t- . . ."

I fling myself at him and faux-bawl.

"Oh, now, now . . . is it really worth all *that*?" Father coos, patting my back. "We'll work it out. You'll see. Everything's going to be fine. Just fine."

I smile. There will be no homework for me.

8. My Mother Says It's My Fault My Homework Ate My Homework

"Good! The ferret's back in the cage," Mother says, coming back into the room.

"Fur!" Abalina says.

"Yes," Father says, "the fur is back in the cage, but, sadly, not before he chewed up our scholarly eldest daughter's mathematics homework."

My mother looks at me. I do my best to look devastated.

"Well, you'll have to redo it," she says.

I gasp. *Redo* it? I can't redo it! School starts on—"

"We've been down this road, Mother," Father says. "Apparently, Zaritza is overwhelmed with other work."

I let him take care of this.

"No, no, no," Mother says. "Zaritza volunteered to watch the ferret, and she let him escape. It's her own fault he ruined her homework."

"Can we talk about this without blaming?" I ask. I've overheard her say that to father when they argue.

"This is not about blame. This is about natural consequences."

"Duh!" Abby says, looking like she's about to cry. She doesn't like the arguing.

"Now look what you did," I say to my mother. "Now the baby's crying!"

"I thought we weren't blaming?"

"Why don't I take our younger daughter into the other room?" Father says, and takes Abby from my mother and heads for the door.

"Father!" I call after him, but he's already out of the room and shutting the door behind him. The coward.

"Sit down with me, Zaritza," Mother says, and pats the bed.

"Why? Are we going to have a talk?"

"Sit," she says more sternly.

I sit.

"Zaritza, how many times do I have to remind you that when you neglect your responsibilities you must face the consequences?"

"And how many times do I have to tell *you* that I don't like responsibilities, or consequences?" I pinch my eyebrows together, which I know wrinkles my forehead, making me look filled with despair.

"But you are showing so much more independence these days," Mother says. "You help in the kitchen, and you clean your room. . . ."

That's true. I don't mind helping in the kitchen when it means chopping or mixing or stirring. But I don't like the washing or drying or putting away. I do *not* like taking out garbage or compost. And I guess I do keep my room pretty clean. It doesn't look like an earthquake hit it, like my friend Wain's does, that's for sure. But then I don't do a lot in here except rehearse in the mirror and sleep. I have a lot of costumes, but I have a big trunk to stuff them into.

"For the most part, you're being a good role model for Abby," she goes on.

"For the most part? Don't I brush my teeth and make my bed? She doesn't even *have* teeth. Or a bed! She doesn't have to do anything. She doesn't even go to the bathroom by herself!"

"She really looks up to you, Zee. I'd like her not to make excuses when she loses something, or blame other people. Like your glasses, or the necklace you borrowed from me?"

It's the old bait and switch. She hooks me with compliments, then starts complaining.

"I'm sorry about the necklace." I cast my eyes down. "I left it in the bathroom. Someone else probably knocked it into the sink. And I've been looking everywhere for the glasses."

"They were very expensive, Zee. We bought them because you need them."

"I know," I say, and slouch. I do feel a little bad about this, even though I know exactly where they are. They aren't lost; they're hidden. I don't want to wear glasses. Actors only wear them onstage, as part of a costume.

"Here's the thing. Bandito already ruined my vacation. Now he ruined my math homework, and I don't want to spend the little time I have left doing math. I want to enjoy my time off. I deserve it."

"But—" she starts to say. I cut her off.

"I'm sure Mr. O. will understand. I'm sure he'll count the homework even though I can't turn it in. What matters is that I did it, right? That I understand it?" Of course, I didn't do it or understand it.

I pause, awaiting Mother's verdict. She musses my hair, a good sign, then stands up.

"You can take it up with Mr. O. after the break if you like. But if you don't get a passing grade this semester, there will be—"

"Consequences. So I've heard."

9. My Homework Won't Eat My Stroopwafels

Mother leaves and, because she doesn't close the door behind her again, Abalina crawls in.

"Zuzza!" she says. "Zuzza! Fur!"

"He's not—oh, never mind. Come here."

I hold my arms out, and she crawls to me across the carpet. Then she rolls back onto her huge, diapered butt. She wobbles when she sits, like she's a gigantic egg turned up on its end. I reach out for her fat little hands and she latches onto my thumbs. The kid has an iron grip.

"Okay, Abalina, stand up," I say, and tug a little. "Uppy."

She pulls my thumbs and rises up to her feet. She's wearing a pale yellow onesie with a picture of a bright red ladybug on it. CUTE AS A BUG it reads in curly letters. Her fat thighs stick out of the leg holes. How will her little feet ever hold up so much weight?

"It's time you learned to walk," I say, and start slowly pulling my thumbs free.

She giggles, then her body folds in the middle. Her diaper swings forward, but, before it hits me, she straightens up and the diaper swings back.

"Dah!" she says.

This is her idea of dancing.

"Yeah, dancing. But I'm going to let go now, Abby, so stop dancing."

She doesn't. She probably only heard the word *dancing* and thinks I'm encouraging her.

"Look, kid, I'm your role model. You've seen me walk, right? Now you do it. It's easy. Ready? *Walk!*"

"Wah!"

"No, with a *K* at the end, Abby—*Walk!*"

"Wah!"

"Fine, have it your way. I'm going to let go. Ready? Wah!"

Instead of letting go, she grips my thumbs tighter. I try a different tactic.

"Clap, Abby!"

She claps, which, of course, means she lets go of my thumbs. I tricked her into standing up by herself. If I tell her she's standing, she'll freak out and fall right on her huge butt. That's what she always does.

But I can't help myself.

"You're standing!" I say, and applaud.

She stops laughing and stands there a second, staring at me with her gooey mouth open. Then she looks down at the floor, and down she goes. Air puffs out of her big diaper.

I clap louder. "Yay, Abby! You stood up!"

She smiles and claps back. "Uppy!"

"Yeah!" I say. "You stood uppy! All by yourself! Want to do it again?"

She stops smiling and points at Bandito's cage. "Fur!" She's changing the subject. She doesn't want to stand up anymore.

"You want to see the fur? Okay, come on."

I hoist her off the ground, stagger over to my desk, and plop her into my chair. She loves riding in my desk chair, so I give her some zigzags and spins on the way to the cage.

"Fur!" she says.

Bandito clucks.

This makes her totally crack up. Her giggling sounds like a machine gun in a bubble bath: *HUH GUH-GUH-GUH-GUH-GUH-GUH-GUH-GUH!* [big breath] *HUH GUH-GUH-GUH-GUH-GUH-GUH-GUH-GUH!* It cracks me up, too.

When we've calmed down, I roll her over to my rolltop desk and take out a box of stroopwafels from a cubby.

"Key! Key!" Abby says.

"I keep telling you they're not cookies. They're stroopwafels."

I hand her the box, then roll her back to the cage.

"I know you didn't eat my stroopwafels," I say to Bandito, as I pull one out of the box. "I know there was nothing left in my pocket but crumbs."

"Key!" Abby says with her hand out. Her arms are so short. They barely reach over her head.

"I don't know about giving you a cookie. It's close to dinnertime."

She tilts her head and makes a little pout.

Maybe I'm her role model after all.

"Peas?" she asks. That's her *please*.

"Okay, but only one."

Now, like I said, stroopwafels are expensive, almost a dollar each, which is why my parents won't buy them for me. I have to buy them myself, with my own money. I don't get an allowance, so I have to rely on money I rake in from relatives on my birthday and Christmas and stuff. My mother makes me put most of that in a bank account for college, but she does graciously allow me to keep a tiny bit of my own money to buy things I need, like stroopwafels.

I'm not crazy about the thought of wasting one on a baby who would be just as happy with a Nilla Wafer, so I break one in half. Then I break it in half again and hand her a piece. A quarter of a stroopwafel is more than enough for a baby. She snatches it in her iron grip, stuffs it in her mouth, and starts sucking on it.

I stuff the other quarter through the bars to Bandito. I don't know why. Maybe to entertain Abby. Maybe because I feel bad that I accused him of stealing from me when I knew he didn't. If someone did that to me, I would be so mad and would demand at least a quarter of a stroop-wafel.

Bandito creeps cautiously toward it, sniffs it, knocks it around with his paw, then turns and creeps away.

I can't say I'm disappointed. I prefer he doesn't like stroopwafels. And I like the way he made Abby and me laugh. Maybe he's not so hideous after all.

10. My Homework Ate My Acting Career

It may be a new year, but it's the same old *school* year. I'm still in fifth grade, I'm still behind, and Mr. O. is still being difficult.

"I appreciate your taking good care of Bandito," Mr. O. says, "and I'm sorry he ate your homework, but I can't give you a passing grade in math without the completed assignments."

"But it isn't *my* fault my homework ate my homework!"

"That was amusing the first time you said it, Zaritza," he says without laughing, or even smiling, "but it doesn't explain why Bandito was *able* to eat your homework. How did he access it? If he was out of his cage, he should have been with you, under your supervision. How could he have chewed through pages of math homework without your noticing?"

"He's fast! He just—*zzzoom!*—got my note-book and before I could stop him—*chomp! chomp! chomp!*—chewed it to bits!"

"If that's true, why didn't you simply redo the assignments? Considering you'd already completed them, doing them again should have been a snap." And he snapped his fingers.

Mr. O.'s a pretty nice teacher, but he gets like this: logical, detail-oriented, nosy. Like a lawyer. Or a mother. He can never just accept what I tell him and leave it at that.

"I didn't have time! Bandito ate them *yesterday!*" Which isn't true, but what difference does a day or two make? "Then my baby sister, Abalina, got very ill. *Really* ill." I almost said "deathly ill," but stopped myself. I feel bad enough pretending Abby is sick, when she isn't. "We're not sure what it is yet. But my sick, crying baby sister definitely affected my ability to concentrate."

I stare off into the distance. Staring off into the distance is good when you want to look like you're really upset about something. It's like you're so upset you don't even notice reality. Actually, I was staring at Bandito, who didn't seem happy to be back at school. I was with him on that.

"So you don't have your homework, which you promised to turn in today, because the ferret ate it," Mr. O. says. "And you didn't redo it because your sister got sick. Is that your story, Zaritza?"

"No, it's not my *story*. It's the truth." Though it isn't.

"I'm sorry, then," he says, shaking his head. "No credit for the homework."

"Listen," I say, and lean forward and set my palms on his desk. "Why don't you just tell me what I have to do, and I'll do it."

"Your homework," he says, then he blinks three times. Blinking three times is Mr. O.'s way of saying you knew what he'd say before you asked. "Including the assignments I give you today."

"I mean, *besides* doing my homework. Can't I do some extra credit or something?"

"Extra credit is available only to students who have turned in all their work."

"You were going to let me use watching Bandito over the break as extra credit, and I didn't have all of my homework turned in."

I knew when I started that sentence it wasn't going to work out, but thought I'd see where it led me. In a way, I had him, because he broke his own extra credit rule, but in another way, I didn't have him, because he broke his own extra credit rule making a deal that was supposed to help me.

"It was only going to be extra credit if you finished your homework, Zaritza, which you didn't do. But I'll give you till Friday to turn in your work. *All* your work. The homework you didn't finish and the new homework. You'll receive no higher than a passing grade for the past due homework, but you can score higher on the current homework, of course, if you complete it on time. You can work during recess and lunch. I'm happy to find you a tutor if you want. And, of course, you can work on it at home."

I blinked at him five times, my brand-new way of saying I thought he was crazy.

"I was thinking something more like washing

the whiteboard for a week. You know how much I hate washing the whiteboard."

I think it's fun, actually. I just pretend to hate it. That's called "reverse psychology." You pretend to hate things you like so the adults will use it as punishment. It doesn't work very often, but it's always worth a shot in a desperate situation. Like this one.

"Zaritza, you should know something," he says, looking at me seriously.

"So that's a 'no' to the whiteboard washing?"

"As you know, the Laramie Traveling Children's Theater Troupe is coming to our school to stage a play with our class next week."

Know? "Of course, I know! I've been counting down the days all year. I can't *wait* to land the lead role in this year's production. I've already watched the movie *Calamity Jane* four times."

He just nods at me. And that's when I get what he's telling me. The horrible thing he's telling me. I clutch my heart and howl, "No!"

Everybody looks up at me.

"I'm afraid students with non-passing grades are not allowed to participate," Mr. O. whispers.

"And without the math homework, you won't pass."

"You don't mean it! You're joking, right? Tell me you're joking!"

He blinks three times.

11. My Homework Ate My Loyalty to My Teacher and My Faith in My Principal

"Doesn't he know the show will flop without you?" Wain asks.

"Apparently not," I say. "I ask you, what does math have to do with theater?"

Wain shrugs sympathetically. He sits next to me in class and is a big fan of my work. He sees himself as an actor, too, but knows that one day I will be a big star of stage and screen and that, at best, he'll play supporting roles.

I don't mean to be mean. Wain is just pretty ordinary. He has ordinary short brown hair, and an ordinary face, and an ordinary voice, and ordinary charisma. He even dresses ordinarily.

About the only thing unordinary about him is his name, Wainwright, but, of course, he goes by the more ordinary Wain.

"You *must* be in the play," he whispers, his eyes shiny with devotion.

I consider asking him to let me copy his homework, but Mr. O would see right through that old trick. Wain's penmanship is tiny and perfect, while mine is bold and sweeping, like me, and the movie *Titanic*.

Besides, it would mean having to write out all the answers for all the assignments. That's a lot of answers. Plus I'd have to show my work—or, in this case, Wain's work.

"No, we'll have to come up with something else."

"So what do I do?" I ask.

"How about we go over Mr. O.'s head? Take it up with Ms. Tsots. She loves the arts."

Ms. Tsots is pretty arty for a principal. She wears sparkly cat's-eye glasses and colorful vintage dresses. She has a bumper sticker that says ART SAVES LIVES, which I don't really get. I mean, exactly how does it do that?

"That's not a bad idea," I say.

"Come in, Zaritza!" Ms. Tsots says like I'm her niece and she hasn't seen me in ten years. She's like that with everyone. Perky and positive in an over-the-top way. I think it's a performance. No one's like that in real life.

"Thank you!" I say, just as perky.

"So how can I help you today, Zaritza!" she says with this huge smile. She has a really big mouth, filled with really big teeth, which I'm pretty sure she had whitened. They're as shiny and white as our toilet at home. That's a pretty gross simile, but it's true.

She sits down behind her desk and gestures for me to sit in one of the guest chairs. I do, then go into my pitch.

"I came to tell you how super excited I am about the Laramie Traveling Children's Theater Troupe coming next week, and to say thank you so much for inviting them!"

"You came here to celebrate?" She gasps like adults usually do when I do something good, like it's a big shock to them. "Thank *you*, Zaritza Dalrymple! Thank *you*! It's so refreshing and gratifying to have a student come in here just to applaud one of our programs! Especially one of our arts programs! You know what an enthusiastic supporter I am of the arts!"

"Art saves lives!" I say.

"Exactly! It certainly does! *Thank* you, Zaritza!" She pops out of her chair and walks around her desk to me. "Now please forgive me, sweetheart, but I've got an exceptionally busy schedule this morning, so I'm going to have to scoot you on your way. But, again, thank you *so* much for dropping in to say 'Yay!'"

"There *is* another *teeny* matter I wanted to discuss with you, Ms. Tsots. It won't take a *teeny* second."

"Oh?" She glances at her watch. "Okay, but be quick." She leans back and sits on the very edge of her desk.

I swallow hard, like what I'm about to say is so painful that even speaking about it is difficult.

"It's too bad . . . . . ." I hang my head. ". . . that

I . . . . . . won't be able to participate in the play." I bury my face in my hands.

"Oh, no!" she says. "What a pity. I remember you in *Little Pig! Little Pig!* You have great talent."

"Thank you," I say into my hands. Her compliment sends electricity through me—I *love* praise!—but I hide it. I'm playing grief-stricken here and must stay in character. "You see, I'm . . . well . . . a bit behind in my math right now . . . and so Mr. O. has decided I can't participate in this once-in-a-lifetime theatrical event if I don't catch up." I peek up at her, pitifully.

"I'm certain Mr. Osojnicki made his decision fairly. He's a fine teacher. And classwork does comes before special programs. . . ."

"I offered to do extra credit. I took care of the class pet all during my winter break. And I really did my best to make up the work. Really, I did! Unfortunately, Bandito—he's our class pet, a ferret—well, he . . ." I choke up. ". . . he chewed up my math homework!"

I try producing faux tears, but I feel too rushed,

so I consider trying the my-homework-ate-my-homework line on her. It didn't go over so well with Mr. O. It sounded rehearsed, which made it sound like an excuse. A lie.

I glance up at Ms. Tsots. She's showing signs of ending this discussion and leaving. I decide to give it a shot. It can't hurt.

"That's right," I say, shaking my head with faux disbelief. "My homework ate my homework!" Then I sell it with an exaggerated, palms-up shrug.

"HA!" she blasts so loud I almost swallow my tongue. "You are too much, Zaritza Dalrymple! Too . . . much!"

That's more like it. Ms. Tsots gets me.

But then she stands up and straightens her skirt and her smile vanishes. "I'm sorry, Zaritza, but this is your teacher's call. Now I really must get to my meeting."

I go blank. Not on purpose. I'm not acting. I'm truly devastated.

I store the feeling away for later use.

"We do have tutors, you know," Ms. Tsots says, holding the door open for me.

Tutors, tutors—that's all I hear! Tutors won't do my homework for me.

Or will they? *Hmm.*

"Thank you, Ms. Tsots," I say, walking past her. "I'll look into that."

Wain, waiting in the office, leaps from his chair.

"So?"

I say, "So I need a tutor."

12. My Homework Tutor Ate My "My Homework Ate My Homework"

I was assigned Eden as a tutor. She's in Mr. O.'s class, too, though I've never said boo to her. She's really quiet, and I'm really not. She's also super smart, even smarter than Wain.

I don't get why anyone would choose to spend recess in the library helping other students with their math. Even smart kids need fresh air and exercise, right? Does she have something against fun?

I'm only here because I have no other choice. If I want to star in the play, I have to do my homework. Or get it done for me.

"Hi, Eden!" I say with a big faux smile.

"Hi, Zaritza," she says. It's like Eden inhales when she talks. She also doesn't make eye contact. She cast her eyes downward and steals little peeks, like she's checking to see if you're still there. Even then she doesn't look me in the eyes. Maybe she's afraid of people. Doesn't she know she's one, too?

Her not looking at me gives me time to study her. Maybe one day I'll be cast against type and play a character who is painfully shy. I notice the pinched lips, the curved shoulders, the crossed arms, the hands tugging on the ends of the sleeves of her sweater. All good stuff that might come in handy someday.

Eden is Asian, by the way, though she speaks perfect English and doesn't have an accent. I'm pretty sure she was born in America. She has jet-black hair that hangs straight down and looks like she cuts it with a paper cutter. *THHHOOOMP!* She dresses like an American—no kimono or sari or anything. Every day she wears a leggings-skirt-top ensemble; in cold weather, she adds a sweater. The one she's wearing now is taupe. Her colors are always drab:

brown, gray, beige, taupe. Like a mouse. She's actually a lot a like a mouse: small, drab, shy, nervous. Are mice smart?

She doesn't wear rings, necklaces, or bracelets. Personally, I love bangles and wear so many of them that my biceps are buff. Eden does wear one item of jewelry: earrings. I swear, everyone's ears are pierced but mine. Even drab, mousy Eden has pierced ears, and she wastes them on plain silver studs.

She opens her math textbook. "Which assignments do you need help with?"

"The last eight. Plus today's."

She briefly looks into my eyes, just long enough to show me how shocked she is that I would let myself get so far behind. Then she starts flipping pages in the book.

"So that would be . . . let's see . . . pages two hundred thirty to . . . two hundred sixty-two."

That's a lot of pages. More than fifty? Ugh.

"I did do them, you know," I say, "but I was caring for Bandito in my home when my baby sister left the cage door open, and Bandito got out and—"

"Your homework ate your homework?" Eden says with a little grin.

I can't believe it. My homework tutor ate my punch line! And her timing was *so* off. I want to give her the stink eye, but I need her, so I don't.

"Yes! Ha! Good one! I didn't know you were *funny.*"

Her face blushes, and when she tries to hide it, she pokes her pencil into her nose.

"Careful there!" I say with faux concern. She deserved that poke for trampling my line.

She blushes redder and covers her face with both hands. "So, you did the homework?" Her lips squeeze into a pucker when she talks. "You understood it."

"Ummmmm . . . sure, yeah, of course."

She lowers her hands. "Then you don't need a tutor. You can redo it."

"Rrrrrright. Exactly. But who has the time? Not me. My life is so scheduled. *Over*scheduled, really . . ."

"You can work on it right now." She pivots the book so I can read it. She offers me her pencil, the one that was in her nostril. Yuck. "Since you've already figured out the problems, it shouldn't take long. I find the challenging part of math to be figuring out *how* to solve problems, not actually solving the problems."

"Really?" Smart people say weird things.

"You could probably finish at least one assignment each recess, plus a couple during lunch. You could come here after school, too. I bet you'd be done in a couple of days!"

She's actually looking at me again. I'm stunned. She stays after school to tutor? Does she not have a life?

I do.

"I can't stay after school. I have too much to do. So many . . ." (I hate using the R-word, but . . .) ". . . responsibilities. You have no idea. Plus I need to prepare for auditions. You know the Laramie Traveling Children's Theater Troupe is coming next week, don't you?"

I wouldn't be surprised if she didn't. Her life is based on math, not art.

"Yes, I do, and you don't need to worry about the auditions." She tucks her chin, likes she's embarrassed again. "You're such a good actress."

"That's very kind of you to say." I heard a famous actor say that during an interview on an entertainment show. I can't remember which actor or which show, but I remember the line. *That's very kind of you to say.* It's a good way to sound humble when someone compliments you. "The problem is, I can't participate in the play unless I finish this homework."

"I see," Eden says, but I don't think she does. She seems really confused, like she can't relate to not getting to do something because of home-work. She's so smart she finishes it at school. "So you have nothing to worry about, right? Just do the assignments and turn them in, then you can participate."

I lean in and use my *this-is-serious-so-really-listen* voice. "I. Don't. Have. The. Time. What I was thinking was you could help me. You could read out the answers and I could write them down. It would go so fast that way."

She straightens up and her head tilts to the side, like a chicken's. Her dark eyebrows gather over her eyes like storm clouds. "I . . . I don't think I can do that."

"Sure you can. We can start now and probably power through the rest over lunch. So, page two hundred and thirty, problem number one . . ."

She's still in the weird chicken-neck pose— her ear is practically touching her shoulder— only now she is starting to shake her head.

I jump in with, "Being in this play is the most important thing in the world to me, Eden. It's everything. Acting is my life."

She sucks in the corner of her mouth and chews on it. I can tell she's asking herself questions, maybe wondering if giving me the answers is cheating. So I repeat, more urgently, "Acting is my *life,* Eden!"

She leans forward onto her elbows and gives me a *this-is-serious-so-really-listen-especially-since-I'm-very-shy-and-looking-at-you-this-directly-is-difficult-for-me* look. Then she looks down at the table.

"I'm sorry, Zaritza. I can't give you the answers. I'm sorry. I'm really sorry."

"So you're sorry then," I say, and stand up.

This is called a parting shot. Storming off comes next, and I pull it off perfectly. Each heavy footstep is perfectly stomped. I can feel everyone in the room looking at me, thinking I'm bad for stomping in the library and for getting angry at poor, shy, helpful Eden. I don't mind one bit. At least they're looking at me.

Calamity Jane was always blowin' her top and hollerin' and stompin' off. And slammin' the door, too. Unfortunately, the library has automatic sliding doors, so all I can do is storm up to them, wait for them to slide open, storm out, then wait for them to slide shut. If I were directing my life, I'd have put real doors there. But I'm not. I'm a kid.

Still . . . a good scene.

13. My Homework Ate My Best Friend's Homework

"Wait—shouldn't you be doing your math instead of watching a movie?" Wain asks as he points the cursor at a picture of a singing Calamity Jane, dressed up in a fringy, brown buckskin outfit. "Not that I'm against watching a movie."

Wain is definitely not against watching movies. He watches them all the time. He's one of those kids, like Eden, who finishes his homework in a matter of minutes, then reads a book while the rest of us suffer. Because he doesn't have to do homework after school, he gets to watch movies on his parents' computer. He calls it research, training for his career as an actor. A supporting actor, that is.

If you watch a movie with him, he drowns it out telling you all the other movies the actors in it were in before. It's "Oh, that's the guy who played the bad guy in *Blah Blah Blah*" or "That's the lady who played the queen in *Blahbity Blah*" or "That kid played the main character's girlfriend's little brother in *Blahbity Blah 2*." It's annoying, but I appreciate that there are kids like Wain who will be keeping track of my movies when I start making them. I have to admit, he knows his stuff. I learn a lot listening to him. But I still have to sock him sometimes to shut him up.

Like now.

"Ow!" he says, rubbing his arm. "What was that for?"

"For asking me that. You know I don't need to know math to be a great actor. I need to study this film so I can nail the audition and play the lead in *Calamity Jane*."

"But if you don't make up your math assignments, you won't *get* to audition," Wain says.

I sock his other arm.

"Stop it!"

"Then shut up. The movie's starting."

"My mom says you're not supposed to hit me," Wain says, crossing his arms in front of him so he can rub both sore spots at once.

"You're right," I say, casting my eyes downward. "I'm sure sorry, Wain. It's just . . ." Just what? I don't know. Dramatic pauses are also good for stalling till you think of an excuse. "I'm just sorry. Start the movie."

He scowls at me but does what I ask.

The movie starts with Calam (that's what her friends call her) singing from on top of a stagecoach that's flying across the prairie. When they get back to Deadwood, where Calam lives, she goes into the saloon and orders up a sasparilly.

I stand up, hook my thumbs under my armpits, straighten my spine and my neck into one long stick, swivel my head quick like a bird, and say, "Barkeep! A sasparilly!"

Wain gives me a thumbs-up, then says, "The guy who plays Wild Bill Hickok was in *Seven Brides for Seven Brothers*, remember? Howard Keel. He was in *Kiss Me, Kate*, too, which was based on Shakespeare's . . ."

"Shhh! I cain't hear the pi'cher!"

"I think I'll try out for Wild Bill," Wain says, looking a bit wounded.

Wain play Wild Bill? He's not the Wild Bill type. Wild Wain Wexler? Nah. More like Plain Wain Wexler.

Even though that's not a bad joke, I don't say it. I don't want to hurt his feelings. Wain's pretty sensitive.

"Sure," I say. "Sounds good."

Luckily, Calam runs at her horse from behind and springs up onto its back. What an amazing woman. What an amazing character.

"I'm tellin' ya, I was born to play Calamity Jane."

"I agree."

"No, I *need* to play this part, Wain. This part will make me a star." I give him a serious look. "Where's your math notebook?"

"You want to copy my homework?"

"I don't see any other way."

He nods, like he sees I'm right, but I can tell he doesn't want to do it.

"You don't have to," I say. Though I'm really hoping he will.

He pauses the movie.

"If I let you, it's just this one time," he says. "And it's just so you can audition."

"Of course, of course," I say. "I've totally learned my lesson. I'll never need to ask again."

He takes a deep breath and lets it out real slow. His conscience might ruin this for me.

"Never mind," I say, and set my hand on his shoulder. "I understand." I'm not sure if he'll buy this, but sometimes pretending to give up makes someone give in.

Sure enough, he digs his notebook out of his backpack.

"Here," he says, not looking at me. "Today's is in there, too."

"*Nine* assignments to copy? Are you kidding me? My homework will give me carpal tunnel!"

14. My Homework Ate My Quality Time with My Father

I won't do all the homework at once because, one, it hurts my wrist too much, and two, Mr. O. might think I cheated if I showed up tomorrow with it all finished. He might even test me to see if I really knew how to do it. I have a few days before I have to turn it in, so I'll pace myself, turn in the homework a little at a time. That will help my wrist, too. I'll need it to play Calam: to snap reins and twirl pistols. I might even need to throw faux punches. You can't do any of that with a bad wrist.

"So how's it going with the math?" my father asks at the dinner table.

"Fine," I say.

He faux-furrows his brow. "Can you be more vague?"

"I've done two assignments. Only seven to go . . ."

"Don't forget, you'll be getting new homework each day," Mother adds. "So you'll have *ten* due by Friday."

"Thanks for reminding me." I push my plate away. "I just lost my appetite."

"You need to work on it tonight," she goes on. "Right after dinner. Nothing but math till bedtime."

"But that's not fair!" I bang my fist on the table. "All I do is math. It just isn't my thing. *Drama* is my thing!"

"No kidding," Mother says under her breath.

Abalina grunts, then bangs her fist on the table. It hits her spoon, which sends the peas in it flying. One lands in my milk.

My father cups his hands around his mouth, making a megaphone, and announces, "Step right up! Step right up! Try your luck at games of skill! That's right—games of skill!"

"One pea in a glass wins!" I chime in.

My mother leans her head onto her hand and wilts.

"Mother, why don't you go in and rest?" Father says. "You've had a trying day. Our eldest daughter and I will clean up in here. Right, eldest daughter?"

"We will?"

Father elbows me.

"I mean, we *will*!"

Mother nods, then climbs slowly to her feet.

"That's it!" Father says as she plods out of the room. "You go in and lie down and leave everything to us."

"You're welcome, Mother!" I call after her.

"It's not easy being a stay-at-home parent," Father whispers to me after Mother is gone. "I know. I stayed home with you."

Which is probably why I'm fun and a good actor, and not a grump like Mother.

Poor Abby.

She's sitting in what we call her director's chair, which attaches to the table. It's like a real director's chair, only it's small and doesn't have legs. When Abby sits in it, she looks like she's floating above the ground. It used to be mine when I was little. I bet it was fun to sit in it. Now I'm too big, and my feet reach the floor.

Father stands up and starts clearing the table, so I help. I don't even wait till he asks me, like I do with my mother. It's more fun cleaning up with him. He makes it fun.

"After we clean up d'is mess, we gotta set up ten tables," he says with a New York accent, like the cab drivers in movies. He faux-chews a wad of gum. "Big convention in town. Extoyminatahs, I hear."

"I heard it was teachahs," I say, getting into the act.

"Heh. What's duh diff'rence?"

We faux-guffaw.

"When we're done heeah, I can help you with d'at homework a' yuhs. I'm not too shabby at math. I got all the way up to the t'oid grade, you know."

"I was t'inkin' mebbe we could watch a movie tuhgedda tonight. Whaddya say?" I nudge him. "I'll buy ya a box a' popcorn. I hear *Calamity Jane* is playin' in da livin' room."

"Gee, d'at would be swell! But is it suitable for a baby? Ain't d'ere a lotta shootin' an' guns an' whatnot?"

"D'ere is. It prolly ain't appropriate fer young'uns."

"Tell you what. I'll put d'is one to bed while you finish up in here. Deal?"

"Deal."

He leaves with Abby, and I go back to the table for more dishes.

That's when my mother walks in.

"No movie," she says. "Not till your math is done."

"But I *did* my math, Mother! Remember? All day!"

"No movies till you're caught up. Responsibilities before fun."

"Watching *Calamity Jane* isn't fun. I need to watch it to prepare for my role in the play. It's research. It's homework!"

"No movie," Mother says. "Math." And she leaves the room.

I sit down at the table, fuming. I know she's going to go talk to Father. He'll listen to her, too.

We won't watch the movie. I'll spend the night copying Wain's homework instead.

I can't wait till I'm famous. Then I'll write my memoirs and tell the world all about how my mother tried to sabotage my career. I'll make her the villain in my life story. That'll show her.

Father comes into the kitchen, his head hung low, like he's about to tell me bad news. He faux-punches my arm. "Rain check on duh movie?"

15. My Homework Ate My Mother's Trust in Me

The popcorn Father made for me is gone except for some unpopped kernels. I lick my finger and mop up the rest of the salty butter at the bottom of the bowl. Then it's gone. There's nothing to do now but my homework.

I sigh and look at the next problem.

$$14. \quad \begin{array}{r} 191{,}349 \\ -\,144{,}672 \\ \hline \end{array}$$

I know how to do it. I just don't know *why* I should to do it. Don't most normal people use a calculator for problems like this? Who even subtracts numbers like this in real life?

"I put in a hundred ninety-one thousand,

three hundred and forty-nine kernels of popcorn into the popper. A hundred and forty-four thousand, six hundred and seventy-two popped. How many didn't?"

Wouldn't a person just say, "a *lot* of popcorn"? Or even "a ton of popcorn"? How much is a hundred ninety-one thousand, three hundred and forty-nine kernels anyway? Did I eat that many?

This is all Mr. O.'s fault. He's so detail-oriented. I bet he counts every kernel as he fills his popper.

I take out Wain's homework notebook and start copying. I can't simply copy the problems though: I have to make it look like I did them. So, technically, I'm not cheating. I'm acting. I write down random numbers, then pretend I made a mistake and erase them, then write new random numbers, and pretend they weren't right and erase them, too. I do this till I've made a nice gray smudge. That's what my actual work looks like: smudgy. I also doodle a lot, so I draw stars, some with five points, some with six, some with more, but the minimum is five. Less than five isn't a star. It's a square. Or a diamond.

I'm trying to make a star with four points when my mother asks, "What are you doing?"

I scream a bloodcurdling scream, my favorite kind. I don't like them as much, though, when they're real.

"Stop sneaking up on me like that!" I yell, clutching my heart. "You almost killed me!"

"What are you doing?" she asks again. She sounds suspicious.

Oh, right—Wain's homework is on the kitchen table in front of me next to mine. I stand up, blocking the evidence with my body.

"What do you think?" I ask, pretending to be outraged as I reach back and try to slide Wain's notebook under my textbook. "My math. Didn't you say I had to?"

She scrunches her face up like she doesn't believe me.

"Okay," I say, slouching like I'm about to come clean. "You caught me. I was *doodling.*"

"You're copying Wain's homework."

"*What?* How dare you? I'm insulted! I mean really!"

She reaches around me and snatches Wain's

notebook, then she holds it up in my face so I can see the name *WAIN WEXLER* written on the front.

I'm ready for this. "You think I'm copying his work? I'm not copying it. I'm *consulting* it. It's something we do in Mr. O.'s class. When we need help, we *consult* another student who understands it. In my case, that's usually Wain."

"Wain's not here, Zaritza," Mother says, and turns to leave—with Wain's notebook! My ticket to the auditions!

"Where are you going with that? Wain entrusted that notebook to me, not you."

She stops and slowly turns around. Mother can be a drama queen herself sometimes. You can't live with my father and me without it rubbing off.

"Do your homework, Zee. Your *own* homework."

"But I was consulting—"

"You will come home directly from school tomorrow and work on it. You will do nothing in your free time except math until you have caught up. That means no movies. No Wain. No drama. Do you understand?"

"But—"

"Do you understand?"

I plop down onto my chair as if all my bones have turned to jelly. I'm a jellyfish in a chair. "Yes."

"And you are *never* to copy the work of another student. It is wrong and you know it. If I ever catch you doing it again, I will take away all your theater privileges. That means no plays, no acting classes—"

"What?" I shriek.

"—for the rest of the school year. *And* you and I will need to sit down with your teacher and have a conversation. You could get suspended, you know—"

"Okay, okay! I get it! Will you stop yelling?"

I hate it when she gets so mad. It's like homework. It makes it hard to breathe.

She plops down onto the chair next to me, closes her eyes, brings her hand up to her forehead, like she's taking her own temperature. I bet it's over a hundred.

Finally, she opens her eyes and looks at me. "So do you need help?"

I give her a naughty puppy face. "Yes."

She leans over to look at my textbook. "Show me where you were before you started copying Wain's work."

"Are you kidding? I have to go *back*?"

16. My Homework Ate My Freedom

It's now Thursday night. I've done more math in the past three days than all the days in my whole life put together.

I start right when I get home from school and have to sit in the dining room so that my mother can check that I'm not cheating or fooling around. There is nothing in the dining room but a table, some chairs, my homework, and me. Mother keeps Abalina and Wormy out and periodically brings me "brain food," which sounds like something you feed brains, not people. It's actually carrots, walnuts, apples, and ants-on-a-log (raisins on peanut butter on celery sticks). I don't eat ants. I'm not an anteater. I don't eat logs. What am I, a beaver? I flick off the raisins and lick out the peanut butter. She also brings me water, but not too much. She doesn't want me "rushing off to the bathroom every other minute," as she puts it.

In other words, I'm in math prison. Mother is the warden. She even sends me out to the backyard for five minutes of exercise. I'm not allowed to call anyone or have visitors. I'm dying of boredom and loneliness. And math. I'm dying of math. Math is killing me. Math should be in prison, not me.

I miss Wain. I miss Abby. I miss fun. I miss movies. I miss Father. I even miss Wormy. That's how desperate I am. And lonely. I hate being alone. There's no drama when you're alone.

There's just math.

I did math with Eden during lunch and recess. She's pretty patient. I would never put up with someone as fidgety and complainy as me. I tried a million ways to get her to do the work for me, but she saw through all of them. She's pretty clever. I kind of wonder if the shy thing is an act. Let's face it, we all act, especially when we want something.

Eden's technique is to suddenly look you straight in the eye and not look away or blink till you do what she wants. Because she usually avoids looking you in the eye, this technique is especially effective. When you try to get her to look at you, forget it, but then—*voom!*—her black eyes turn on you and freeze. They pin you like a butterfly collector pins a butterfly to whatever it is that they pin butterflies to. Butterfly boards. (Butterfly collectors are warped.)

"I want you to do this problem," she said today, pointing her long, dainty finger at a problem that wasn't assigned. It was even, and I only have to do odds.

"I don't have to do that one. I'm not doing extra."

She pinned me with her eyes. "I want you to do it without a pencil. I want you to do it in your head, then tell me the answer."

"Why?"

"So you can see how good you've gotten at this."

I agreed, but only so she'd stop staring. It made me uncomfortable.

I added the numbers, carried, then answered, "Forty-eight thousand, eight hundred and twenty-one."

"Remember how hard problems like that used to be for you?"

"You mean yesterday?"

She smiled real big. Her teeth are really straight and white, and I bet they're not whitened, like Ms. Tsots's.

I have to give the girl credit: she's good. I wonder if she's ever acted on the stage. She'd be good as a best-friend sort of character. If she weren't so shy, she could audition for the play.

"Are you working, or daydreaming?" my mother asks, peeking into the dining room.

I snap back to the dining room. To my prison cell.

"I'm working, warden," I say.

17. My "Dog" Ate My Homework

"We should celebrate!" Father shouts at the breakfast table.

"No shouting at the breakfast table," Mother says, looking at him like he's crazy.

He is crazy.

I love crazy.

"You want to celebrate her catching up on her long overdue homework? And after I caught her cheating?" Mother asks, then suddenly bends over and snaps at Wormy, "No begging! There's food for you in your dish!"

Wormy gloomily robot-walks away. Even "dogs" are actors.

"Could we have a movie night?" I suggest to Father while Mother's distracted. "How about a double feature: *Calamity Jane* and *Calamity Jane*. I really need to study it."

"I'll whip up the popcorn, pardner!" Father says in a cowpoke drawl.

"No movie till today's homework is done," Mother growls.

What a grump she is this morning. I bet Abby kept her up. I wouldn't know. I can sleep through a tornado.

"Did you keep Mommy up last night?" I ask Abby.

My mother doesn't like this. I get the feeling she wouldn't like anything this morning.

"It's Friday, Mother," I remind her. "We don't get homework on Fridays."

"We better get going, Zaritza," Father interrupts, setting his half-empty coffee cup into his bowl of half-eaten oatmeal. He never eats all of anything. Maybe that's why he's so skinny.

He puts his dishes in the sink, then lifts Abby up into the air. She's wearing her onesie with the pictures of ice cream cones all over it. No wonder she can't sleep. The kid loves ice cream.

"Bye, Baby Abby," he says, and burrows his

pointy face into her flabby neck. Abby giggles like a maniac.

"Bye, Duh!" she squeals.

I bus my dishes, too. "I ate all my food," I say to the room. "I'm a growing girl."

"You are indeed," Duh says. "You'll be as tall as your mother in no time.

Really? I like the thought of that. Heh, heh.

"Did you put the permission slip in your backpack?" she asks.

She means the permission slip for the play next week. We had to get permission to miss normal classes so we could participate. Did I pack it?

"Of course I packed it!"

I leave the kitchen and scoop up the permission slip from the dining room table where she put it out for me.

"You didn't remember," my mother says from the kitchen. *How does she do that?* "Do you have your math?"

My *math*! How could she think I could possibly forget the homework I labored over for days?

"It's in my backpack," I yell.

I get my backpack, unzip it, and rummage

around for my math notebook. I don't find it, so I dump the contents of the bag onto the floor.

"Check your room," Mother calls from the kitchen.

I rush to my room. It's not on my desk, the beanbag chair, or the bed. It's not under it, either. I don't see it. I start to panic.

"Mother!" I scream. "Where's my math?"

There's no answer. She enjoys it when I can't find what I'm looking for. She loves crossing her arms and giving me the *if-you-ever-put-things-away-where-they-belong-this-wouldn't-happen* look. I'm glad she's in the kitchen.

Except that I need her help.

"MOTHER!"

Abby crawls into the room.

"Have you seen my math notebook, Abby?" Yeah, I'm asking the baby for help. I'm that desperate.

She turns her head and stares into space. She looks like she's thinking.

"You *have*, haven't you? Where is it, Abby? Where's Zuzza's notebook?"

Her eyes wander back to me. Slowly. Tell me this kid isn't a drama princess.

"Wum," she says.

"*WHAT?!*"

My scream is so loud it tips her over onto her back.

"Where is he, Abby? *Where's . . . Wormy?*"

She looks toward the door.

I leap over her and run into my mother. Literally.

"Where's Wormy?" I yell.

"Slow down . . ."

I dodge my mother and run down the hall. "Wormy! Wormy! Where are you, you little cyber-dog!" I'm starting to cry. For real.

I collide with my father in the dining room.

"No rugby in the 'ouse, mate," he says in a passable Cockney accent. Cockney is not one of his best.

"Must . . . find . . . 'dog'!" I pant. I'm totally freaking out, but I do the finger quotes.

"'E's in the sitting room, dearie. Your mother banished 'im, poor widdle f'ing."

A wave of complete and utter terror washes

over me. Wormy doesn't like being scolded by Mother. (I know how he feels.) I remember he even walked right past his food bowl.

I race to the living room and find him under the coffee table with what is left of my math notebook in his tiny, machinelike jaws. A new word, *wormicide,* flashes in my red-hot brain.

"Give it to me, dog!" This time I skip the finger quotes.

He growls and scoots back away.

"GIVE ... *IT*!"

He yelps at the sheer power of my voice, and the notebook drops from his mouth. He runs away. I lift the tattered remains of my hard labor.

It's now truly true: My "dog" ate my homework.

Mr. O. will never believe me.

18. My Homework Could Eat My "Dog" That Ate My Homework

"Catch him!" I scream as I run through the house. "Catch him! I want that 'dog'!" I'm hysterical, furious, crazed, but I finger-quote.

My mother is yelling, "Calm down!"

My father is yelling, "Let's go!"

Abby is yelling, *"WAAAAAAAH!"*

I outyell them all: *"ME . . . KILL . . . WORMY!"*

It sounds bad, I know, but all I can think of are those long, boring hours, adding and taking away, multiplying and dividing, carrying and borrowing, and how in a matter of minutes that hideous . . . *THING* . . . ripped it all to shreds. Which means I won't get a passing grade. Which means I CAN'T BE IN THE PLAY!

I don't care how it sounds. I'm going to kill me a Maltipoo.

"Where ARE you, you coward!" I yell.

"Zaritza," my father says, approaching me with the notebook in his hands. He's cradling it like a baby to keep it from snowing confetti on the carpet. "I'll go with you to talk to Mr. O. I'll explain that you truly did do your homework, and that Wormy did in fact feast on the fruits of your labor. We'll show him the mangled mess." He holds it up. "Mr O. will understand. Your work won't have been in vain. You *learned*, and that's the important thing." Then he sets his hand heavily on my shoulder, gazes deeply into my eyes, and adds, "Wormy doesn't have to die."

A funny sound bursts out of my mouth, part grunt, part guffaw. He got me on that one. It's amazing how laughter can put out anger, like water on a fire.

My mother steps between us. "Go! You're late!" She's holding Abby, who's still bawling.

"Mother, you don't look well," I say. "Try to get some rest today."

She growls like a mad dog. Which only makes her look worse.

"What's wrong with Mother anyway?" I ask my father in the car on the way to school.

"I think she's tired of being at home. She wants to get back to doctoring."

"So why doesn't she?"

"We don't want to send Abby to day care just yet."

"Did you act grouchy like that when you stayed home with me?"

"Absolutely not. But to be safe, you should get a second opinion. Ask Mother."

"You guys should have stopped when you were ahead. Abby causes nothing but problems."

"I agree. Mother and I want to return her, but we can't find the receipt."

"You could get rid of Wormy. That would definitely make life less stressful. . . ."

And I get an idea. What if I were to bring Bandito home again, and what if I left the cage door open again, and what if Wormy was in my room at the time, and what if my door was closed and he couldn't get out. . . .

I'm still mad at Wormy.

Father did smooth things out with Mr. O. The homework counts. I will get a passing grade. I get to star in the play!

The troupe arrives on Monday, three days from now, and they will be here all week, every day, preparing us for the performances. That means five days of acting class instead of normal class. I'm so happy about it I can't stand it. Or sit still. Mr. O. keeps telling me to, but I can't. I'm way too excited.

Finally, he sends me to the library. Bad kids have to be escorted down the halls at our school by good kids, so he sends Eden with me.

"Congratulations on finishing your math homework," Eden whispers in the hall. "I knew you could do it."

"Yeah," I say in a normal voice. I figure I don't have to whisper, being the bad kid. "I couldn't have done it without you, though."

"Of course you could have," she says even more quietly. She's trying to turn my volume down.

"The best part is I get to play Calamity Jane in

the play." I'm talking even louder than before. No one turns me down.

"Can you be quieter in the halls, please?" a voice from behind us says. We turn and see a teacher poking her head out of her classroom.

"We're very sorry," Eden says, assuming, I guess, she gets to speak for both of us.

"Sorry, ma'am," I say with a Calam twang. "'Spect I'm feelin' plum rambunctious! Ah'll try to keep my big yap shut." And I give a big exaggerated nod.

The teacher frowns and pulls her head back into her classroom. Eden crumples like someone has pulled out her spine.

"See what I mean?" I say proudly. "I'm a natural Calamity."

"Yes, I do see that," she says.

19. My Homework Ate My Baby Sister . . . . . . Almost

"Fur!" Abalina says when Father and I carry in the cage. She's thrilled.

Mother isn't.

"Are you crazy? After what happened last time?"

Why did I bring Bandito home again, even though he kept me up for two weeks with his chattering and his stench, even though he ate my homework? Was it for revenge—so I could sic him on Wormy? That's what gave me the idea, but that wasn't why. The real reason was that I felt bad for him having to spend the weekend at school all day by himself. He liked it at my house. He liked Father. Abby liked him. Maybe I was starting to as well.

"I couldn't help it." I say. "He loves me."

"In our defense, we *did* call," Father says, sounding like Mother is *his* mother, "but it went to voice mail."

"I was napping with Abby."

"Oh, good!" He kisses her cheek. "So you caught up on your sleep."

She growls at him. She growls a lot. I wonder if she might be a werewolf. That would be so cool.

"Come on, Father," I say musically. "Let's put this in my room. It's heavy."

We leave Mother fuming behind us and set Bandito in my room.

"I better go start dinner," Father says. "Your mother looked hungry."

"Yeah—for human flesh."

"I was thinking trout. Isn't this Friday?"

Father always cooks fish on Friday. "Mother's Night Off," he calls it. In the summer, he grills the fish outside. But when it's cold, like now, he uses the broiler.

"Can I have some trout for Bandito?" I ask.

"Sure. Broiled or raw?"

We both look at Bandito, who is slithering around his cage like a hairy snake.

"Raw," we say at the same time.

In the kitchen Father cuts a piece of the bloody trout and sets it on a plate. We look at each other and faux-gag, then I take the fish to my homework.

Bandito gobbles it up.

I open the Ferret Observations notebook and write, *Loves trout.*

I go back to the kitchen.

"He loved it."

"Oh, I yam zo proud zat zee muskrot eez cone-tent!" he answers. This is his French accent, and it's better than his Cockney one.

"Can I have another piece?"

"*Oui, oui,* mademoiselle. *Encore* trout for zee muskrot! *Toot sweet!*"

He carves another bloody chunk and sets it on the plate, and I head back to my room. I meet Mother in the hall. She's holding Abby.

"Fur!" Abby says. "Beh!"

"No, the fur is in the cage, Abby, not on the bed."

"Is that our trout?" Mother asks.

"Just a little piece of it." I don't tell her it's the second little piece of it.

"Didn't your teacher send ferret food home with you?"

"It's an experiment." Which is sort of true.

"Zuzza," Abby says. "Uppy!"

"Can you take her for a while?" Mother asks. "She can watch you feed the ferret our fish."

"Nice alliteration, Mother. Come on, Abby."

I can't carry her, since that takes both arms, and I have to carry the fish, so I take her chubby hand and she toddles along beside me.

"See that you don't let the ferret out," Mother says, wagging her finger at me as she walks away.

The woman needs a vacation.

"Fur!" Abby says when we finally reach my room. (Babies are so slow!) She points at the bed.

"He's not on the bed, Abby," I say. "He's in his—"

But he isn't.

I let go of Abby's hand, and she collapses onto

her cushioned butt. I rush to the door and shut it.

"Fur!" Abby says. "Beh!"

She starts crawling for my bed. I scoop her onto my beanbag chair—I don't want my homework to eat my baby sister—then peek under the bed. I see him hunkering behind whatever all that stuff is under there.

"Give up, mustelid. There's no way out."

He clicks at me, then hisses, but stays where he is.

"Come out and I'll give you another piece of fish," I say, faux sweetly.

Where did I set it? I don't remember putting it down.

"Beh!" Abby says.

"Yes, you were right. Congratulations. Now where's the fish?"

"Fiss," she says, and points at the plate, which is on the floor behind me. The fish isn't on it.

"Did he sneak out and take the fish, Abby?"

"Shoo!" Abby says.

This one throws me. Is she telling me to go away?

"Shoo?"

"Fiss. Shoo!"

Is she shooing away the fish? I'll be glad when she starts speaking in complete sentences.

"Fish shoo?" I ask.

She points at one of my shoes, which is laying nearby. I pick it up. The trout is inside. Gross. How did it get there?

Doesn't matter. I pluck it out, set it on the plate, then rub the fish juice off my fingers onto the carpet. Fish juice. Gross.

"Here it is," I say to the fur under my bed. "Here's the fish. I bet you can smell it. Now come on and get it." I smile like I'm not furious at him.

He doesn't come out.

So I wait.

And wait.

And wait.

I'm role-modeling patience.

"Do you see how patient Big Sister is being?" I say to Abby.

"No," she answers.

She obviously didn't understand the question.

At last, Bandito starts creeping toward me, slowly at first, but then—*zoom!*—he slithers right at me. I scream and jump back, and he shoots by me.

He stops in the middle of the room and starts prancing around, his claws making little ripping sounds on the carpet. He's not running away. He's not attacking. I think he's playing. Performing. Putting on a show. He bends his long back, then snaps himself open, which propels him forward, like a Slinky pull toy. I'm afraid Abby might choke from all her giggling. I'm laughing, too, mostly because of Bandito's huffing and wheezing. It sounds like laughter. Either that or asthma. I'm pretty sure we are witnessing the weasel war dance. Probably because of the fish.

He darts under my rolltop desk and then out and under my nightstand and out and under my chairs and out and back under the desk. He's gone crazy. He falls over a lot as he scrambles around, but he just barrel-rolls himself back upright. He's acting a lot like a kitten, and I really like kittens. They're cute and frisky. I've only seen Bandito in his cage, or hiding in my parka, or in my desk, or being held by someone. With a little room, he's, well . . . kind of adorable. And dramatic!

When he finally calms down, he comes over to me and sniffs at the plate. Then he peeks up at me, like he's asking for the fish. Politely.

"It's all yours, fur," I say.

He picks it up with his pink fingers and starts chewing on it, like a squirrel eating a nut.

I sure have a lot to enter into the Ferret Observations notebook.

20. My Homework Ate My Name

"They're here!" I shout. A white van is parked in the lot. On its side, in colorful, sparkly, fancy letters, are the words LARAMIE TRAVELING CHILDREN'S THEATER TROUPE.

"Just one van?" Wain asks. "It all fits in one van? The directors, the sets, the costumes?"

"There's probably more coming." I'm a little annoyed at his negativity on a such a positive day, the day, in fact, I've been waiting for all my life. If I'd known he was going to act this way, I wouldn't have suggested we pick him up on the way to school. I would have let him walk.

We get out of the car, and Father calls out, "Your caged beast, m'lady?"

He means Bandito. I really had fun with that

silly mustelid over the weekend. I'm actually a little sad I have to bring him back.

"Help my father with the cage, will you, Wain? I need to get inside."

"Uh . . . sure," he says.

"Actually, Your Ladyship?" Father calls after me. "I was rather hoping you and your man-servant, Wain, might tote the cage inside, if it's not too much bother, as I must away to duties on another campus."

"Oh, all right!" I suppose even the biggest stars must sometimes perform normal, human tasks, even on the most important day of their lives.

When Wain, Bandito, and I enter our classroom, there are two young strangers standing with Mr. O., a man and a woman. It's obvious they are not from Bridge's Creek, that they're from Laramie, that they're professional theater people. I drop my end of the cage onto a stray desk and head over to them.

"Hey!" Wain gripes behind me.

"Howdy! I'm Zaritza!" I say with as much Calamity Jane spunk as I can muster. I stick out my hand to shake. When they stare blankly at me, I add, "Welcome, thespians!"—which is a fancy word for *actors*. This isn't very Calamity-like, but I've been rehearsing it for months and can't not say it.

The lady speaks first. She's wearing glasses with lime-green frames, a plaid jumper over a white blouse with puffy short sleeves, and neon pink kneesocks. Her head is tangled into spiky red dreads. She's definitely an artist. I mean, she's not even wearing makeup. And her blouse is wrinkly, like she slept in it.

"You have a ferret," she says with a faux smile, then yawns. "Did she sleep well last night? Is it show-and-tell today?"

"Is that what it is?" the man says. "A ferret? I thought it was a skinny possum."

He's shorter than the lady but is better dressed. He's wearing a dark green blazer and black pants, and shiny black leather shoes, though they're scuffed. Under his blazer he's wearing a red T-shirt with the same logo that was on the van. I can see it because his jacket is unbuttoned and his stomach is a bit rounded. He has a little pointy beard, though no mustache for some reason.

Doesn't a beard make it hard to play different

characters? Dreads, too, I bet. Maybe these two aren't actors. Maybe they're directors. Or *casting* directors. Maybe they're just the ones who'll be auditioning us.

"Please take a seat, Zaritza," Mr. O. says. "We'll have introductions after the announcements. It's going to be a full day."

"Yes!" I say. "A day filled with drama and comedy and tragedy! Of *theater*!" I rehearsed that line, too.

"Sit down, Zaritza," Mr. O. says again.

What a buzzkill he is. But at least he said my name. Twice. That should help them remember it.

"Okay, Mr. O.," I say, then, as an aside to the theater pros, I add, "We'll talk later." I part with a finger-gun-shot and a hard wink.

They laugh a little. They get me.

Sitting through the Pledge and the announcements is misery, way worse than usual. Then, at long last, things get started.

"As you all know, this week we are delighted to have the Laramie Traveling Children's Theater Troupe with us—"

Loud cheers erupt, mostly from me.

"—who will be guiding you through the step-by-step process of putting on a stage play."

"A *musical* stage play," the Laramie guy adds.

"Right," Mr. O. says. "This project will take place each morning till first lunch, which means normal morning activities will be canceled—"

Really loud cheers erupt, and hooting, too. I love to hoot.

"I thought you'd like that," Mr. O. says with a grin. He probably likes it, too: it means he gets a break from us. "We will still meet here after lunch, of course. Remember, you are not required to participate in the play. If you don't wish to, I will find something for you to do here in the classroom."

Right. Like who would choose not to participate?

"Those of you who do choose to participate, I expect you to be attentive, courteous, respectful . . ." And *blah, blah, blah* until at last . . . "And so please let me introduce you to your directors, Josh and Hannah."

We all clap, but I make sure I'm the loudest, and the last one to stop.

"Hi," Hannah says, giving us a little wave.

She's blushing and uncomfortable, so she can't be an actor. Actors love an audience. "I'm Hannah—with an *h* at both ends—and I'm one of your theater facilitators, and I'm so super excited that together we're going to put on a *show*!"

That was totally canned. I bet she says it every time. But I cheer and hoot anyway. It can't hurt to be on her good side.

"A *show*! Woo-hoo! All *right*!"

Mr. O. glares. I stop.

"I'm your director for the play," Hannah goes on. "I'm also stage manager. I coordinate the lighting, the sets, the costumes, and the props. Do any of you know what a prop is?"

"*Prop* is short for *property*," I say. "And it's the objects actors use during a performance."

Hannah nods, then yawns, and her partner steps forward.

"I'm Josh. I'll be your acting and singing coach. I'll also be acting in the play with you, playing the role of Wild Bill Hickok."

I glance at Wain and watch him slump in his chair. I tilt my head, faux-pout, and mouth, *Sorry!* It's better this way, though. No sense Wain getting his hopes up when he didn't have a chance of landing the role.

"I'll be onstage with you at all times during the performances," Josh says. "That way, if you get stuck and can't remember your cues or lines, I can help out. How's that sound . . . *co-stars*?"

He's going to be onstage at all times? Doesn't that make *him* the star? That can't be right. *I'm* the star.

I raise my hand.

"Ah! We have a question," Josh says with a smirk. "What is it, Ferret Girl?"

The class explodes in laughter.

"I'm *Zaritza*, remember?" I say, but my stupid classmates are too loud.

Someone starts chanting, "Ferret Girl! Ferret Girl! Ferret Girl!"

Oh, no! It's becoming a thing! I must stop it!

"Ha!" Josh says. "Ferret Girl has a following!"

No! It's like a nickname. Ferret Girl—with capital letters.

The chanting continues: "Ferret Girl! Ferret Girl! Ferret Girl!"

My homework ate my name.

21. My Homework Ate the Most Glorious, Stupendous Day of My Life

We follow Josh and Hannah to the cafeteria. The tables are all folded up and rolled away. Some of the boys in my class take advantage of all the space and start racing around, acting like apes, as boys often do.

Josh steps up onto the stage, which is only about a foot off the floor, and says in a commanding voice, "Attention, company!"

Good projection. He must be an actor. I like that he calls us "company." Very professional.

"I need everyone's attention and concentration at all times. If I do not have your attention and concentration at all times, I will send you back to your classroom."

The ape-boys deflate like leaky balloons.

"And remember: always walk when you are in this room, unless you are onstage, of course, and I tell you to do otherwise. Anyone who runs will be sent back to the classroom. Understood?"

Everyone nods.

"When I say 'Understood?' I want you to answer, 'Understood!' Understood?"

"Understood!" we all say.

"Good. Now when I say 'Action,' I want you all to stand up and walk to the back of the room. I want you to walk as if you are crossing deep, wet sand. Your feet should sink in with each step. Show me how well you can pretend. Ready? Action!"

I glance around and see some of the kids walking like they have glue on their feet. Wrong. Or they drag their feet, like zombies. Also wrong. I'll show them how it's done.

I take a step and imagine my foot being sucked into the sand, then salt water pouring on top of it. I pretend to lose my balance as I try to tug my foot free. I wobble. I almost believe this is really happening, right there on the hard floor of the cafeteria.

This is what school is supposed to be like!

I look up, waiting for Josh to single me out, but he's not looking at me. He's whispering to Hannah, who is writing in a spiral notebook.

This is part of the audition!

Because I've done such a realistic job of walking in deep, wet sand, everyone else is way ahead of me, so I start walking fast—not running—in deep, wet sand. I move in a squat, like those guys who danced with bottles on their heads in the musical *Fiddler on the Roof.*

"Are you a crab on the beach, Ferret Girl!" Josh howls, which gets a big laugh. The whole cafeteria is filled with echoing meanness.

"Okay, now everybody turn around and come back," Josh says, "only now you're walking on scalding hot desert sand. Emphasis on *walking.* Action!"

Everybody starts hopping on their toes across the floor, saying, "Oooh! Oooh! Hot! Hot!"

"Do we have shoes on or are we barefoot?" I

yell, because I want to get this right, but I can't be heard over all the faux yelping. So I scream louder, "DO WE HAVE SHOES ON OR ARE WE BAREFOOT?"

"Please do not shout, Ferret Girl," Josh says in his commanding voice.

Everyone freezes.

"That goes for everyone. If you have a question, raise your hand."

"But everyone's raising their hands," I say, which is true. For some reason that's what people do when their feet are burning.

"Ferret Girl, if you can't stop shouting out, I'm going to have to ask you to return to your classroom."

Total silence. Everyone looks at me. Usually, that's a good thing. But not when you're in trouble.

What is going on here? Can I do nothing right? This was supposed to be the most glorious, stupendous day of my life. Instead it's the worst. And who is to blame?

"Understood, Ferret Girl?" Josh says.

There is my answer.

"Understood," I say.

22. My Homework Ate My Audition

"I want you each to come up onstage and say your name loudly and clearly," Josh says. "Loud enough to be heard at the back of the room, and clear enough to be understood. That is how we speak when onstage. Understood?"

"Understood!"

"When you're up here, I'll ask you to do a couple of things. Do them the best you can, then go back and sit down and be a good audience member. Polite and attentive. Understood?"

"Understood!"

"You," he says, pointing at Melodie. "Come up and tell us your name in a loud, clear voice."

Melodie goes up and says, "Melodie," in an unloud, unclear voice.

"Okay, Melodie," Josh says, "I want you to recite something you know by heart."

"Recite something?"

"That's right. It could be a poem, or a nursery rhyme, or a scene from a movie you like. Anything."

Melodie thinks a few seconds then recites "Hickory Dickory Dock." Which is pretty easy and lame. And she gets stuck halfway through.

But Josh says, "All right! Amazing! Thank you! Now, Melodie, can you sing something for me?"

"Sing?"

"Yes, sing. Anything you know. Anything you like."

She blushes. "All right." Then she croaks out "Row, Row, Row Your Boat."

"Excellent!" Josh says.

Oh, come on. What's his standard for excellence?

"Now I'd like you to pretend to be a gorilla, Melodie," he says.

"A gorilla?"

I knew she was going to say that.

She acts like a gorilla, which to her just means

going "woo-woo-woo" while scratching her side. But Josh eats it up.

Then he calls up Aaron, who recites the Pledge of Allegiance, sings "Row, Row, Row Your Boat," and has to pretend to skate on cracking ice. Then Opal recites the Pledge of Allegiance, sings "Row, Row, Row Your Boat," and pretends she's surfing. After Tristan recites the Pledge of Allegiance and sings "Row, Row, Row Your Boat," Josh says there is to be no more reciting the Pledge of Allegiance or singing "Row, Row, Row Your Boat."

Wain recites his favorite scene from his favorite movie, *Napoleon Dynamite*. Of course, he doesn't play Napoleon, the lead role. He plays Pedro, the supporting one. He knows his place.

Josh laughs and claps, then asks Wain to do the scene again, only this time with the hiccups. Wain gives it his best shot, which isn't too bad. Then he sings "Forever Young" till Josh stops him.

"Thanks, Wain, that'll do," he says.

Eden recites a poem about creatures with green heads and blue hands who went to sea in a sieve. (What's a sieve?) Then she sings "This Little Light of Mine."

Josh makes a huge fuss over it, clapping loudly and saying, *"Brava,* Eden! Well done! "

Then he asks her to pretend she's in class and knows the answer to her teacher's question but is too shy to raise her hand. Ha! Being shy doesn't require acting for Eden, so she does this easily.

"Excellent, Eden! Just excellent!"

Her name he remembers.

What Josh is asking us to do are pretty basic acting exercises. Not many of my classmates have ever acted before. I have, so I can't wait for my turn. Wouldn't you know it that I have to wait till Josh calls everyone else up first? Guess he's saving the best for last.

"Anybody else?" he says, looking out at us.

I don't budge. No way am I going to admit that he overlooked me.

He didn't, did he? He *couldn't* have!

"Oh—Ferret Girl! Come on up!"

I stand and walk through my snickering classmates toward the stage. I don't rush, but I don't dawdle. I walk, like a queen—a drama queen—to center stage and cast my eyes at the middle of the audience. I don't make direct eye contact with any one person. This is what my acting teacher, Paul Dalrymple, says I should do. (Who better to teach me than an experienced stage actor like my father?)

"My name . . . . . ." I say, then pause to create some anticipation.

"Is Ferret Girl!" Aaron yells.

My classmates laugh themselves senseless while I wait for Josh to do the right thing and scold Aaron for yelling out, like he did to me. But he doesn't scold him. He *laughs*.

"I thought yelling out wasn't allowed!" I say, and cross my arms. "That's just . . . unjust!"

Josh coughs into his fist, trying to disguise his laughter, then says, "Okay, let's calm down, everyone. Let's show some respect."

I wait for quiet, but the whispering and chuckling continues.

"Go ahead," Josh whispers to me. "Don't be afraid."

Afraid? To speak in front of an audience? *Me?* What an upside-down day this is!

I say my name with good tone, resonance,

volume, and clarity, only instead of saying Zaritza Dalrymple, I accidentally say *Fa*ritza Dalrymple. Everyone totally loses it. They roar with laughter. Even Josh is snickering. Wain isn't, but I can tell it's difficult for him.

"I mean *Za*ritza," I say over the laughter. "*Za*ritza Dalrymple."

Aaron bellows. "Hi, *Fa*ritza! *Fa*ritza, the *Ferret* Girl!"

"Quiet now!" Josh says. "I mean it. Aaron, one more outburst and you will spend the week in your classroom."

Everyone shuts up.

"Okay, Zaritza, will you recite something for us? Something short, I hope." He peeked at his watch. "We're running late."

I take a cleansing breath. "I'm going to do a scene from *Calamity Jane*," I say, "the classic 1953 movie musical."

"Sorry, but can you do something else?" Josh says. "I don't want anyone to audition for any specific roles in the play."

I stare at him. "But I've been rehearsing the role for months . . ."

"That's great, but I'd like to hear something you haven't rehearsed, if you don't mind. Do you know anything else by heart?"

Do I know anything else by heart? Of course I do!

"Of course I do!" I say, insulted. "I can recite . . ."

But I can't think of anything to recite. Not one scene. Not one rhyme. Nothing. I notice Hannah is writing something in her notebook. Something about me not remembering things? Like my own name, maybe?

"I can do a scene from *The Sound of Music*." It's always a good idea to do something from *The Sound of Music*. Everybody knows it, even if they don't really like it.

"That's fine," Josh says. "Sing a song from it."

"But shouldn't I recite first?"

"It's getting pretty late, so just the song, please."

"Okay. I'll do 'Do-Re-Mi.'"

"Perfect," Josh says.

I sing the song up through fa, then get stuck. I can't remember the next note!

"That's fine. Very nice. Thank you," Josh says.

"But I'm not finished."

"It was enough."

Hannah writes something else in her notebook. Probably *Can't remember simple songs everybody in the world knows. Doesn't know the musical scales. No memory at all, apparently.*

"Now what shall I have you pretend?" Josh says, scratching his little beard. "I've got it!" And before he says it, I know what it will be. I start to shake my head, but he says it anyway: "Let's have you pretend to be a ferret!"

He lets the laughter fill the room before asking my backstabbing classmates to simmer down.

"Now, you know all about ferrets," he says to me. "What interesting things do they do?"

"Well," I say, "they do a war dance."

"A war dance?"

"Yes. A weasel war dance."

Josh grins very wide. "All right then! Let's see what one looks like!"

A part of me says I should storm off the stage, but another part—a much bigger part, the part of me that lives to act—tells me to stay right where

I am, where I belong, onstage, and do what my director tells me. The show must go on. Show the people what you got. Act your heart out.

I close my eyes and think of Bandito, tearing around my bedroom last night, doing his dance. Though I'm mad at him for all the pain and torment he's caused me, I can't help smiling. If I do it right, I can get the kids to laugh *with* me, instead of at me.

I bend over and set my hands on the stage. I arch my back as high as I can. I start huffing and wheezing and saying, "*Dook! Dook! Dook!*" Then I start hopping around. I fall over on my side and quickly spring back to my feet, like Bandito does. I hop and skip and flip and huff all around the stage until Josh says, "Okay, Ferret Girl! That's enough! Very nice!"

I break character. I am me again. I stand up straight, look out at the audience, and bend forward at the waist. They are laughing hysterically, and I feel it is with me, not at me.

I exit, stage right, pass back through my chuckling classmates, and sit down next to Wain, who is stifling laughter.

"Are they laughing with me or at me?" I ask in his ear.

He doesn't answer. He looks at me with a guilty expression.

They're laughing at me.

23. My Homework Ate My Dignity

"You were good," Wain says. "Really."

When people add "Really," they usually mean "Not really."

"That ferret has ruined my life."

"I can't believe you actually said 'Faritza'! You've got ferrets on the brain."

"Not just me! Stupid Josh won't stop with the Ferret Girl thing. Why didn't he call you Ferret Boy? You were carrying it, too."

He shrugs. "The main thing is you did a good ferret, and you showed Josh you speak loud and clear."

"Really? That's the main thing? Not that everybody laughed at me, or I said my own name wrong?"

"The guy's a pro. He goes all over doing these shows. I'm sure he can spot real talent. He would be an idiot to not cast you in the lead."

"That's very kind of you to say. You were good, too."

"I was really hoping to try out for Wild Bill," he says.

"It's weird Josh is playing such an important character. And he wouldn't let me audition for Calam!"

The bell rings and Mr. O. calls us in. Recess is over. Josh and Hannah spend it inside choosing the cast. I'm nervous to see if I got the lead. Excited, too. I run to get in the line going inside.

"No pushing, *Faritza*," Aaron says loudly, though I didn't touch him.

Only a couple of kids laugh. I hope this means the joke is wearing off.

Josh and Hannah are in the cafeteria, sitting on the edge of the stage, their feet on the floor. I rush over and sit down in front of them.

"Walk, please, Faritza," Hannah says to me.

"Sorry, *Fannah*," I say.

"It's Hannah," she says.

"It's Zaritza," I say.

"Okay," Josh says when the others are seated. "We've chosen the cast." He waves a fat stack of papers over his head. "Please come up for your script when I call your name. At the top it says what role you'll be playing, onstage and off. That's right, some of you will be stagehands as well as playing roles in the play."

Are you kidding me? I may have to move scenery? Will the indignities never end?

"I know you'll want to talk to your friends about what role you got, but I'm asking you to please observe the silent concentration rule until all the scripts are handed out. I'll go quickly. Then we'll take a very short break so you can talk. Understood?"

"Understood!"

"So, Aaron, Bianca, and Cooper, please come on up."

Curses! He's going in alphabetical order by the first name. Wouldn't you know it?

Aaron, Bianca, and Cooper collect their scripts, glance at them, and sit down.

Wain leans over and whispers to me, "They don't seem too excited."

"The names of the characters probably don't mean anything to them," I whisper back.

Hannah gestures a silent *shhh*! You can barely even breathe in here without getting in trouble. It's worse than being in class.

Eden goes up with the next group, and when she reads what's written on her script, she makes a tiny little hop—just a quick lift up onto her toes and back down. What could it have said that would make shy Eden light up like that? Knowing her, she's probably just an extra, but also gets to be ticket taker. Something that requires plenty of math. She sits back down, clutching the script to her chest as if it were a teddy bear.

Then again, Josh sure did like her poem, and her faux shyness (which wasn't faux).

After Jacqueline gets her script, she sits back down beside me. I peek over and see, handwritten at the top in red ink, the words DEADWOOD LADY #2 + STAGEHAND. Not only is she playing a character without a name (read: extra), she's not even the *first* Deadwood lady. She's Lady #2.

"Opal, Sam, Tristan?" Josh calls out.

They get their scripts and sit down. Nobody seems particularly thrilled about what's written on them. Except Eden, that is.

"Vivian, Wain, Xander?"

"Good luck," I whisper to Wain as he stands up.

When he comes back, he drops his script in my lap. PA CANARY + CHORUS is written at the top. He's playing Calam's father—who died when Calam was a teenager—and singing in the chorus on musical numbers. On the front page of the script is the list of characters. There's CALAMITY JANE; MA, PA, LIJE, SILAS, and LENA CANARY; WILD BILL HICKOK, CAPTAIN CRAWFORD, COLONEL CUSTER, and some names that look like Indians: RUNNING DEER, WINTER WREN, and SITTING DUCK. Maybe Eden is playing an Indian. That would make sense. She looks kind of Native-Americanish. But all the Native American roles are small. I doubt landing one would make Eden go up on her toes.

Wain suddenly elbows me and hisses, *"Zaritza!"*

"Try Ferret Girl!" a boy shouts. I think it's Xander.

"Go get your script," Wain whispers.

Josh is waving it at me from the stage.

He must have called my name.

I leap to my feet and run to the stage.

"Sorry," I say as I snatch the script.

My eyes fly to the top of the page. Written there are the blood-red words DEADWOOD LADY #3 + CHORUS.

24. My Homework Ate My Chance at the Big-Time

"Come on, *tell* me," Wain says. "I mean obviously you're not Calam, but who are you? Are you Ma Canary? Are you Colonel Custer?"

His idea of a joke, but I don't laugh. I could easily play George Custer. I just show him my script.

"You're *kidding*," he gasps.

I snatch the script back. "Shut up, will you?" I say. "You want everyone to know my shame?"

"Well, everyone is going to know eventually."

He's right. Why should I hide this indignity? They've seen all the others. Today has been Let's Embarrass Zaritza to Death Day.

"*Jacqueline* has a better role than me! And

she recited the ABC song! And got it wrong!"

"Do you have lines?"

I flip through the script and find a few high-lighted lines here and there, no more than five or six. I look up at Wain, my eyes flooded with real tears.

"I don't get it," he says. "How could this happen?"

"Oh, I *get* it all right. It's the ferret's fault. Ferret Girl. Faritza. My homework ate my chance at the big-time."

I storm away, dramatically, Wain hot on my heels.

I stop, dramatically. He runs into me.

"I want to be alone," I say, with great faux dignity.

He nods. "Okay, but remember: the show must go on."

"Let it go on without me," I say, which is a good line.

I spin on my heel and head for the door. On the way I pass Eden. She is smiling and showing people her script. I stop.

"Hello, Eden," I say as if nothing in the world

were eating me alive. "So what role did you get? Are you taking tickets? Or designing the program?"

Inside my head, a voice is repeating, *Don't tell me you're playing Calamity Jane, don't tell me you're playing Calamity Jane, don't tell me you're playing . . .*

"I'm playing Calamity Jane!" she squeals. Like a piglet. "Can you believe it?"

I swallow my pain. "No. I can't. Congratulations."

"Oh, thank you, Zaritza! I know how much you wanted this part. You really should have it. I've never even acted before. This is just so—"

She stops talking because suddenly there is a very loud growling sound. It's coming from me, from somewhere deep inside me, and I can do nothing to stop it.

"Are you okay, Zaritza?" she asks.

"Me? No, actually, I'm not! You see . . ." I see a blinding flash. I'm sure no one else can see it. It's a flash of rage caused by indignity and unjustness. Then I go on. ". . . *I* am supposed to be Calamity Jane. *I* was born to play her. *I am* Calamity Jane!

Not you. You are not an actor. *You* have never acted before. *And* you are *Asian*! Calamity Jane wasn't Asian! Who ever heard of an Asian cowgirl? It's ridiculous! You can't be Calamity Jane! *I'm* Calamity Jane. *I* am."

"Zaritza," a soft voice from behind me says. A hand is touching my shoulder. I spin round, ready to take the head off whoever's there. It's Wain.

"She's upset," he says to Eden. "I'm sure she doesn't mean it."

"Don't tell me what I mean. I know what I mean. I—"

I stop because I suddenly realize how deathly quiet it's gotten in the cafeteria. I look around and no one is talking. Everyone is looking at me.

"For your information, Asia is a continent," Eden says to me in a shaky voice. "Koreans are Asian. And Russians. And Iraqis. And Indians."

Exactly. She should have been cast as an Indian.

"My family is from Java, which is an island in the Indian Ocean."

"Oh?" I say. I didn't know that. "Where's Java?"

She ignores me. "But my parents were born

in the United States. We're American. Like you. And Calamity Jane. Or do you prefer to be identified by the continent *your* ancestors came from? European, maybe?"

I have no idea what continent my ancestors came from. Or even who my ancestors *were*. My father's from Walla Walla. My mother was born in Iowa. Or was it Ohio?

"Are you saying you're mad at me because I called you Asian?" I ask her. "What should I call you? Javan? Javish?"

She fumes for a second, then blurts out, "I don't see why it matters! Do *you* look like Calamity Jane? She wasn't blonde, you know."

I'm starting to feel bad, and not just because I didn't get the part. It's what she's saying. And she's saying it in front of everybody. I think I might start crying.

"I'm not blonde, either," I say, because maybe if I talk I won't cry. "I'm strawberry blonde."

"Okay, people," Josh says from the stage. "Break's over."

Thankfully, everybody stops looking at me, and starts moving toward Josh and Hannah. I don't. I head for the door. I'm going back to class. Back to Bandito. I'm not going to kill him, though. I'm going to take care of him. Watch him. Take notes in the Ferret Observations notebook. Why? Because I'm not Calamity Jane. Eden is. I'm Calamity Faritza. I'm the Ferret Girl.

25. My Homework Tutor Ate My Starring Role

"Zaritza?" Mr. O. says from his desk. "I didn't expect to see you."

"Me, neither," I say. I walk past him and head for the ferret cage.

"Is everything okay?"

I sit down by the cage. Bandito slithers toward me and paws at the bars. He wheezes. He's glad to see me. He likes me. I like him, too. Except I hate him.

"They call me Ferret Girl, you know," I whisper to him. "And Faritza."

"Are you guys on a break?" Mr. O. asks. "Why are you alone?"

I wish he'd quit with the questions. Can't he

141

see I don't want to talk? Can't he see that my life has ended?

"Maybe you were missing your pal there? You're getting pretty attached to him, aren't you?"

My *pal*? *Attached*? Is he nuts?

"I guess so," I answer.

"What about the play?"

Play? You call that a play? A mouse is playing Calamity Jane, the best actor available is playing a minor character, and the director is in every scene. I don't call that a play.

"*There* you are," Wain says, hustling into the room. "Come on. Rehearsal is starting."

I don't look at him.

"You know," Mr. O. says, "if you don't participate, you have to stay here with me."

I don't look at him, either. Instead I watch Bandito gnaw the bars. He's trying to get out so he can play with me.

"I'll keep you busy doing classwork," Mr. O. adds.

Now I look at him. "Oh."

"Josh is looking for you," Wain says.

"Oh?"

"You really should read the script. Your character has a pretty important scene. You sort of tell Calam off."

"Oh, yeah?"

"I see. You didn't get the part you wanted," Mr. O. says, like this information explains everything to him. Know-it-all.

I turn back to Bandito. "Sorry, but I have to go. You see, the show must go on."

Mr. O. gives us hall passes—after reminding us that we're not allowed to go back and forth from the cafeteria to the classroom without them—and we speed-walk back toward rehearsal.

"Can you believe it?" I ask Wain. "Eden helps with my math so I can be in the play, then she steals my role, and *then* tells me off in front of everybody just because I called her *Asian*. I mean, she *is* Asian, isn't she? Isn't that the right thing to call her? How was I supposed to know she's from Java. Isn't that coffee or something?"

"She's not from Java," Wain says. "Her ancestors are. She said her parents were born in America."

"Whatever. I think she meant all this to

happen. That's why she helped me. So she could embarrass me in front of everybody."

Wain looks at me with his left eyebrow way up, like I'm not making any sense. "I don't think she got mad at you because you called her Asian."

"No? Then why?"

"Because you said she couldn't play Calam because she's Asian."

"She *can't*! An *Asian* Calamity Jane? Java Jane?"

"Quiet in the hall!" a teacher says, poking her head out of her classroom.

"We're sorry," Wain says for both of us. I let it slide this time. After the teacher goes back inside, he whispers, "Eden's right, you know. Calam wasn't blonde. She had raven black hair. I looked it up."

Father once told me that one of the greatest stage actors of all time, Sarah Bernhardt, played Hamlet. Hamlet the *prince*. A man. Actually, in Shakespeare's time (Shakespeare wrote the play *Hamlet*), women weren't allowed to act in plays (how unjust!), so men played all the roles, male and female. Father says what an actor looks like doesn't matter. What matters is how good an actor they are. If they're good, they can convince the audience they're anyone, or anything—like I did in *The Marshmallow and the Frog*. In that play, I *was* a marshmallow.

Another thing Father tells me is that there are no small roles, only small actors. He doesn't mean small like tiny. He means small like . . . well, like I'm being right now. I'm acting like a big baby because I didn't get the role I wanted, and I was mean and spiteful to Eden because she got it instead. Father says every role in a play is important, and any actor, no matter what role they play, can steal the show.

Which is my new plan.

26. My Starring Role Ate My Homework Tutor

"Ferret Girl! You're back!" Josh yells from the stage .

"Yep!" I say proudly. "Ferret Girl is back!"

I've decided to own the nickname, like I did drama queen. Once you own a nickname, no one can hurt you with it.

Wain and I sit down on the floor, and I uncrumple my script. I had twisted it up pretty tight during my little fit.

"Where's the scene?" I say, flipping through the pages.

He leans over and stops me. "Here."

I read from the page. "Deadwood Lady #1 says, 'It ain't proper for a lady to wear trousers.' Then Deadwood Lady #2 says, 'It ain't proper for a lady to say ain't.'" Which is a joke, I guess.

Then Calamity says, "A body who ain't wearin' trousers had better stay inside where there ain't any rattlers, cuz in a frilly frock like yourn it's a lot easier to git bit!" Calam then tries to bite Lady #1.

Then Deadwood Lady #3 says, "That's no excuse for dressing like a man. I've been wearing a dress for years and I've never had any trouble with snakes."

"Ya never rode bareback, neither, I bet," Calam says.

"Of course not!" Lady #3 says.

"And ya ain't ridden into battle, yer pistols blazin'?"

"Certainly not. I am a *lady*, ma'am."

"Then ladies sure miss out on a heap a' excitement!" And Calam fires her gun into the air.

"Firing guns is not what I call fun!" Lady #3 says. "It's dangerous and it hurts my delicate ears."

"I'm awful sorry, ma'am. . . ." Calam says, and bows.

I elbow Wain.

"My character's stuck-up," I whisper.

"Yeah, but she tells Calam off."

"I'd rather be the one firing the gun . . ."

"Quiet, please," Josh says to us. "I want you concentrating on what's happening in every scene. It's important that everyone learns the whole play by heart. You're all essential to making it work."

Yeah, yeah, there are no small roles. But some are sure bigger than others.

I go back to page one and start reading the whole story. It starts when Calamity is thirteen and her name isn't Calamity yet. It's Martha Canary. She and her family are riding a covered wagon from Missouri to Montana. They sing a song called "Ridin' 'Cross the Range." Then Ma Canary dies, and Calamity has to be mother to her brothers and sisters. She sings the song called, "If'n I Put My Mind to It." It goes:

There ain't nuthin' I cain't do,
If'n I put my mind to it.
There ain't no horse I can't shoe,
If'n I put my mind to it.

Obviously, the play is supposed to teach stuff like "Be yourself," "Don't let others tell you how to be," and "You can do it if you try."

Gag.

Onstage, Eden is reading through the song with her brothers and sisters, played by Luis, Cooper, and Devanna. We won't start actually singing the songs till tomorrow, when Aaron's mother comes to accompany us on piano.

"'She was a good woman,'" Eden/Calam says after the song. "'She was brave an' strong an' always took real good care of us. An' she'd want us to be brave an' strong an' keep on goin'.'"

"That was pretty good, Eden," Josh lies. She read it word by word without much feeling or inflection. "But from now on, let's see a little more strength, okay? Remember, Martha's a strong girl with a lot of spirit and a big voice."

"Okay," Eden says in a quivery voice, like she might start crying.

"Okay!" Josh says. "Continue!" He's modeling how he wants her to sound: big. He wouldn't have to model for me. I *am* big.

Next, Calamity slaps her knee and says, "'Now

that's enough of that blubberin'! We got us a ways to go a'fore sundown. Git up into that wagon!'" Eden slaps her knee too softly to hear. And her scolding is too nice. She's too shy to let loose. She sure ain't no Calamity Jane, I'll tell you that.

Josh keeps the run-through moving. The play will only last about an hour when we perform it for an audience, but the run-through takes much longer. All morning.

My scene doesn't come till Calam is a grown woman living in Deadwood. I stand with Ladies #1 and #2 (Melodie and Jacqueline), facing Calam (Eden) and Wild Bill Hickok (Josh). Wild Bill narrates the story directly to the audience as well as appearing in every scene, which means Josh has ten times as many lines as anyone else, which seems totally unjust. The play really should be called *Wild Bill*.

Josh has played the role probably a zillion times, so, of course, he knows his lines backwards and forwards. A lot of his lines are jokes, which he delivers to the audience like a standup comic. After a joke, he pauses for the laugh. I doubt he'll get very many. The jokes aren't funny. Maybe they're for the adults, like a lot of the jokes in computer-animated movies. (I hate computer-animation. I hope by the time I'm in movies the fad has passed. I'm not interested in doing voice work. I want to be seen and heard, not just heard.)

I practice my lines while I am waiting, so when it's time, I say them without referring to the script. I say them loudly and clearly. After the line "I've been wearing a dress for years and I've never had any trouble with snakes," I act terrified that there might be some around.

Josh doesn't comment, but I can tell he's impressed.

"'Ya never rode bareback, neither, I bet,'" Eden reads.

Flat, weak, stiff. But it's my cue.

"'Of course not!'" I say, waving a pretend hanky at her.

"That's good, Zaritza," Josh says.

Yes!

"... but maybe tone it down just a touch?"

No!

"Of course," I say, faux-smiling. "Sorry."

The next scene is a musical number, "Shootin'

Off Your Mouth." The Ladies each a sing a verse, then all of us join in on the chorus. Being Lady #3, my verse is last, which is fine by me. People are more likely to remember what comes last.

After the song, we Ladies are supposed to exit stage right. Jacqueline goes left and crashes into me.

"Careful, Ladies," Josh says.

Lady, I think, but again faux-apologize.

"Good scene," Wain says when I sit down.

"Tell that to Josh."

"I will."

I grin at him. He's my biggest fan. And a pretty good friend, too.

I'll go back up for the finale with the whole cast, but otherwise that's it for me. Not exactly what I had hoped for.

But I won't complain. I am a big actor in a small role.

After the finale, Josh tells us, "Okay, that's it for today. Rehearse your lines! Get together with friends after school if you can. Remember, you must have them memorized by Wednesday. Our first performance is Friday night!"

We're sent out to the playground so the theater can be changed back into the lunchroom. Eden walks off alone, looking pretty upset. She did an awful job and must be feeling discouraged and scared. She just found out acting is no walk in the park. It's hard work, especially when you're the lead.

She looks at me suddenly, like she knew I was looking at her. She flashes me the stink eye and stomps off.

"Looks like she's still mad at you," Wain says.

"Maybe I should help her. She helped me with my math."

"That would be nice of you."

"Yeah," I say, but do I want to be nice to the girl who cheated me out of fame and glory?

27. My Homework Tutor Ate My Parents' Respect for Me

"There are no small roles . . ."

"I know, Father." I don't need to hear the rest.

"Play the role like your life depends on it," he says, sweeping his arm dramatically.

"Her life definitely does not depend on this role," Mother says. "It's just a play."

My mouth falls open. Father's, too. "*Just a play?*" we say in unison.

"Madame, the theater is in our very *blood*!" Father says.

"Bluh!" Abby says.

Father and I laugh. Mother does not.

"Bluh! Bluh!" Abby chants.

Whenever we laugh at something she says, she repeats it over and over until everybody's sick to death of it. She has a lot to learn about comedy. Just because something gets a laugh once, doesn't mean it will again. In fact, usually it won't, unless you change it somehow.

"Lovely dinner conversation," Mother says.

"But she's right," I say. "It's in our blood."

"Bluh!" Abby says.

"That's enough, Abby," Mother says. "Eat your peas."

"Blecch," I say.

"Bluh!" Abby says. "Bluh! Bluh! Bluh!"

Mother glares at me as she shovels peas into my sister's laughing mouth.

"So why do you think Josh cast Eden as Calam, Father?"

"Can she act?"

"No. She's terrible. But she did do a pretty good job reading a poem during her audition. And she doesn't sing too badly."

"He must see something in her. Raw talent. Charisma."

"Bluh!" Abby says.

"Ignore her," I say. "That's the only way she'll stop."

"Maybe Josh gave her the role to draw her out of her shell," Mother says. "To give her confidence."

"Bluh!"

"Abalina doesn't have a confidence problem," Father says.

"Giving her the starring role is more than drawing her out of her shell," I say. "It's more like tugging her out of it and plopping her onstage for nearly every scene and making her sing and cry and yell."

"Poor little turtle," Father says.

"Bluh! Bluh!"

"Eden's Asian, you know," I say.

"So?" Mother says, squinting at me like I said something wrong.

"So Calamity wasn't."

"So Eden can't play Calamity Jane because she's Asian?"

"I once played a worm," Father says. "And you played a marshmallow, Zaritza. Remember?"

"Bluh!" Abby says.

"Eden got real mad at me when I said she was Asian," I say, looking at my lap, trying to convey real regret and shame. It's not entirely faux.

"What exactly did you say, Zaritza?" Mother asks like a cop interrogating a criminal. Now she's mad, too. Boy, this is a touchy subject.

"All I said was that she was Asian and who ever heard of an Asian cowgirl." It does sound mean all of a sudden. Why do things sound so much wronger when you say them around your parents?

"Oh, Zaritza," Mother says, shaking her head.

"Zuzza!" Abby says. At least she's off "Bluh!"

I look to my father for help, but he just looks at his plate. Even he's disappointed in me. Oh, this is horrible! I hate Father's disappointment more than I hate Mother's worst scolding.

"You apologized to her, right?" Mother says.

"Um . . ."

"Immediately after dinner you are to call her and say you're sorry. Understood?"

Now she sounds like Josh.

"Understood," I say.

"You know, Zee," Father says, looking up from

his napkin, "even if you didn't mean to be mean ... well ... it was mean."

Did I mean to be mean? Am I mean person? Am I bad?

I feel bad.

"And after she helped you with your math!" Mother says, rubbing it in.

"You know what you might do?" Father says.

"Yes. I'll call her and tell her I'm sorry, then, if she hasn't already hung up on me, I'll offer to tutor her in acting. Though I doubt she'll want me to. Right now she despises me."

"Maybe the apology will help," my mother says. Then she actually smiles. Wow. We don't see *that* very often these days. She sets her hand on mine.

"Why are you being nice to me?" I ask.

"Because I'm proud of you. You're being a good role model for Abby."

"Bluh!" Abby says.

I laugh. "Think so?"

Mother nods, and wipes a tear off my cheek that I didn't even know was there.

28. My Homework Tutor Is Now My Homework

I didn't call, but that's only because I'm better in person. I need my face and hands—heck, my whole body—to communicate. I pretended to call, though, in a voice loud enough for my parents to hear, and I'll tell Eden I'm sorry today without fail.

I didn't have time to talk to her before school started, and then we were sent to the cafeteria/ theater and were busy rehearsing all morning. Aaron's mother is here accompanying us on piano, so we've been working on the play's songs. Josh broke us up into groups to work on individual scenes. Hannah took some of the groups to talk about moving sets and arranging props.

Every time I got Eden's attention, she stink-eyed me. When we worked on our one scene together, she scowled at me the whole time. She read her lines with more of Calamity Jane's spirit, probably because she was mad at me. She was still pretty awful, though.

I thought I'd talk to her at recess, but she didn't go outside with the rest of us. I don't know where she went, but I guessed the library, to tutor. My next hope was lunchtime, but I couldn't find her in the lunchroom. More tutoring, I bet. The girl's a workaholic. Mr. O. kept us busy in the class-room all afternoon, so my only chance to talk to her was going to be after school.

Which is now.

"Eden!" I say after the bell rings.

She quickly grabbed her things and slipped out the door. I run after her, calling her name. Her shoulders shrink up, but she doesn't look around. In fact, she speeds up. I skip after her. Yes, skip. I've decided the tone of this apology is going to be light and breezy.

When I catch her, I take a deep breath, smile wide, and say, "Hey, buddy! I wanted to say I'm sorry, right? For the things I said yesterday? What was I thinking? It was *so* stupid. I'm really, really, really, *really* sorry. You're going to make an *awe*some Calamity Jane."

She looks confused, or maybe suspicious. I can't tell. Her facial expressions are so . . . expressionless.

"You know I'm not prejudiced or anything. I don't judge people by stuff like that! I never even noticed before that you're . . ." I almost say Asian again.

"Javanese," she says. "Javanese-American, actually."

"Oh, cool. So congrats on getting the starring role! You're doing fantastic."

"You really think so?" she says, frowning. "I think I'm terrible."

"You're not!" I say, though she is. But you don't say that to people, right? Talk about rude. "You know all your lines. Nobody else does, that's for sure."

"You do," she says. "You're so good. You should be Calamity Jane. I don't understand why Josh cast me."

"He must see something in you. Raw talent. Charisma."

"Charisma? Really?"

"Look, Josh wouldn't have given you the lead if he didn't think you could do it. He has a lot of experience, you know. He's a professional."

"But I can't be Calamity Jane. I'm not the right type. Besides, I don't *get* her. Why did she like shooting guns? Or dressing like a man?"

"That's just the way she was. She lived her own way, and made every day an adventure. She loved attention. She loved performing. I think she performed every moment of her life."

I really was meant to play her. Alas.

"See what I mean?" Eden says. "You understand her so well, Zaritza. You should play her."

Here's my chance to offer to tutor her. But before I can, she says, "Would you help me, Zaritza? Would you teach me how to be Calamity? Please?"

I wanted to be the one to suggest it, but I faux-smile and say, "Sure. I'd be happy to."

My homework tutor is now my homework.

29. My Homework's Mother Interrupted My Homework's Homework

"Bigger," I say.

"I can't be bigger," Eden says.

We're in my room, rehearsing. Wain is here, too, and Abby. Wormy is scratching at the door.

"Wum!" Abby says, pointing.

How can a person work under such conditions?

"Everyone can be bigger," I say to Eden. "You're just afraid to. You have to be brave."

"Like the song you sing," Wain says. "'Who Doesn't Want to Be Brave?'" And he breaks into it:

Who would want to be a chicken?
Or a hermit stuck in a cave?
Who wants to be panic-stricken?
Who doesn't want to be brave?

"Bray!" Abby says.

"She's so *cute!*" Eden says.

"I know you're kind of shy," I say, trying to keep her on track. "If you want to be a turtle, that's fine. But onstage you have to come out of your shell."

"I don't want to be a turtle," she says, shrinking up, which is the opposite of what we want. "Am I a turtle?"

"Bray!" Abby says.

Eden laughs. "You're so lucky to have a little sister, Zaritza. I don't have any sisters."

"Forget the sister," I say. "And forget the turtle. It's cornball." Figures. It was my mother's idea, not mine. "What are you afraid of anyway? Are you afraid of screwing up?"

She shrinks more. Bingo.

"You're not going to screw up. You're, like, a genius."

She smiles a little.

"The only mistake you'll make is being too small. It's not like the movies. On a stage everybody looks small, so if you act small, you'll look microscopic. You have to be really big just to look normal-size. You have to be *huge*."

"You!" Abby says.

"Okay, that does it, Abby. We're working in here. You're going to have to stay quiet or you're going to have to leave."

"Aren't you being a little rough?" Wain asks. "She's just a baby."

"Right. And babies don't belong in rehearsal. Be a pal, Wain, and take her out of here. Give Eden and me some time to work alone. Oh, and ask my mother to keep the 'dog' away."

"Okay. Come on, Abby." He holds out his hand.

"Way!" she says, and takes it. "Way" is Abby's version of Wain.

"Don't let the 'dog' in when you leave," I say.

Wain crouches down when he opens the door so Wormy doesn't sneak between his legs.

"No, Wormy. You can't go in there. There's a rehearsal in progress."

He shuts the door behind them.

"Why do you make finger quotes when you talk about your dog?"

"Never mind about that. We need to focus. Listen to me now. You need to understand your character. Maybe if you did, you could be bigger. Calamity Jane was tough. She survived the covered wagon trip that killed her ma. She raised her brothers and sister. When she grew up, she didn't want to be a quiet little lady. She wanted to be a big, loud cowgirl. She didn't want to wear fancy dresses or go to tea parties. She wanted to ride horses and shoot guns and hunt and fight. People laughed at her and told her she was wrong, but she just laughed back and did it anyway. You get it?"

Eden shrunk even smaller.

"You don't have to *be* her, Eden. You just have to *act* like her. When the play's over, you can be Eden again, and the play only lasts about an hour. You can be big and loud for that long, can't you?"

She shakes her head. She looks more terrified than ever.

It's funny. To me, acting is as easy as

breathing, like math is for her. She stuck with me when I was buried in math I couldn't do. She was patient. She waited till I dug myself out. I would be patient, too.

"Say the line, only say it bigger this time. Not huge. Just a little bit bigger. There's nothing to be afraid of. It's just us. You can't possibly mess up, and if you do, I swear I'll never tell a soul. Ever."

She still looks uncomfortable.

"Do it with your eyes closed," I say. "That might help."

She closes her eyes, then opens one and peeks at me, then closes it.

"I'm here. Say the line. Say it big. Rattle the windows."

She takes a deep breath, then says, " 'I ain't never seen such a lily-livered bunch a' no-good yellow varmints in all my born days!' "

It ain't Calamity Jane. More like Calm Jane. Bigger, but too polite.

"Better," I say. "But it could be a lot bigger. And madder. Do it again."

She says the line again, but it barely grows in size. So I tell her to do it again. Then again. And again. Boy, am I being patient. I don't like being patient. A funny thing starts happening: instead of getting bigger each time, she starts getting smaller. I think it's because she's getting discouraged.

I don't know what to do. How can I help her? What is she so afraid of?

A knock on the door startles both of us.

"Who is it?" I snap.

"It's your mothers," Mother says, and opens the door.

"Time to go, honey," Eden's mother says in a tiny, polite voice.

She sounds like Eden, but she doesn't look like her. I mean, she doesn't look Asian—or Javanese, or whatever. She has strawberry blonde hair, like me, and blue eyes. Was Eden adopted?

"Okay, Mama," Eden says, and gets her backpack and coat.

"We've been rehearsing," I say to her mother. "For the play. You're coming right, Eden's mother?" I don't know her name. Eden's last name is Sumarta—which sounds kind of like *smarter*—but since not everybody's parents have the same name as their kids, I don't call her Ms. Sumarta.

"You can call me Melissa," her mother says, rubbing her hands together, like they're cold. "Yes, I'll be attending the play. Come on now, Eden. We have errands to run."

"I'm ready," Eden says.

"Have you ever acted onstage, Melissa?" I ask.

She shakes her head really fast but really small, like the idea of acting frightens her.

Hmm.

"We really appreciate all the help Eden gave Zaritza with her math," Mother says to both Eden and her mother, then smiles awkwardly. It's awkward in here. I don't know why.

Melissa looks at Eden, her eyebrows pinched together.

"Oh," Eden says, then says to my mother, "You're welcome."

"Can Eden come back tomorrow to rehearse more?" I ask Melissa. She makes an expression like she smells something bad all of a sudden but doesn't want anyone to know she smelled it.

"Eden's really getting good," I lie. "Can we

show you one of the scenes we've been working on?"

This freaks both of them out. Honestly, their eyes practically pop out of their sockets.

"Sorry, we really must be going," Melissa says.

Eden jumps up and rushes to her. "Bye, Zaritza. Thanks."

"Yes, thank you for helping her," her mother says. "And thank you, Naomi, for having Eden over."

"Come by any time," Mother says.

Melissa nods then hustles Eden away.

"Wow," Mother says when they're gone. "That might explain some of Eden's shyness."

"Yeah," I say. "It explains a lot of things."

30. My Homework's Homework Scared Her Mother to Death

Day Three came and went. Eden, Wain, and I had gotten off-book—which means we'd learned our lines—but not many others had. Josh tried to get three run-throughs in before lunch and we almost made it. He really worked us hard, but the hardest thing for me was having to sit on the floor and watch others perform. If I'd been the star, none of this would have been hard. It would have been the best day ever.

I did get to be an extra in some of the crowd scenes, and sing in the chorus during the big numbers. The playwright obviously tried to keep everybody involved as much as possible, probably to keep us from fooling around as much as possible.

Josh has been patient and supportive with Eden but has to know by now that he picked the wrong girl. That's nothing against Eden. She just can't do Calam. Josh tried to get her to be gutsier and brasher all day, but nothing worked. Why doesn't he just put me in instead? That's what Eden wants. I heard her tell him so once.

"You're not getting off that easy," he answered. "You'll be a great Calamity Jane. I have total confidence in you."

That's why she and I are here at Eden's house—to rehearse, but first we're having graham crackers and milk in her kitchen with her mother.

"You're lucky you don't have a little sister," I say to Eden. "Or a dog."

She and her mother look at each other, then look down at their plates. What did I say? Did Eden once have a sister or a dog that died tragically?

I dunk my cracker in my milk and it immediately gets soggy and breaks. Half of it sinks to the bottom of my glass.

"I meant to do that," I say. "I like it when

the milk gets all sludgy." Which I definitely don't.

"So, Zaritza," Eden's mother says, "what's your favorite subject?"

"Theater."

"I mean academic subjects. Like math or reading."

"I don't care for either of those. Eden really bailed me out with my math."

"Yes," her mother says, "though I think she could work harder at it."

She glances at her daughter, and Eden squirms.

"I don't think she could!" I say. "She works at it all the time. Even during recess and lunch."

Melissa shifts in her seat. "I have high hopes for Eden."

There's an uncomfortable silence. I don't like uncomfortable silences. I don't even like comfortable ones.

"I do like science," I say, though I definitely do not. "Right now, I'm conducting an experiment on the effects of cow's milk on graham crackers."

Eden snickers, and milk comes out her nose.

"Oh, Eden!" her mother says, and hands her a napkin.

I must remember to never be a mother. Instead I'm going to lead a life of excitement and glamour in a totally napkinless, little-sisterless, Maltipooless, getting-totally-worked-up-over-nothing-less world.

I drain my milk. The cracker sludge slides down the glass and lands on my nose.

"Look at this!" I say, the glass still in my mouth, the goop still on my schnoz. "Fetch the Graham Cracker Observations notebook! *Quick!*"

Eden snorts up more milk. I wonder if she's having the most fun she's ever had. It's the most fun I've ever seen her have.

The fun continues in Eden's room, where I suggest an acting game.

"Let's run lines," I say, "only let's pretend the play isn't a stage musical. Let's pretend it's a . . . scary movie!"

"Huh?" Eden says. "How?"

"Just read your lines, only pretend that you're

in a scary movie, where there's always something *lurking*"—I act spooked—"in the *closet*"—I peek into her closet, then act relieved—"or under the *bed*!" I start to peek under it, then whirl on her and yell, "Boo!"

She jumps and makes a little *Eep!* sound.

"Really? That's your scream?"

She shrugs.

"Let's do the covered wagon scene, before Ma kicks the bucket. Page two, start with 'Pa, we're all . . .'"

"'Pa, we're all outta water,'" she reads.

"No, like you're scared, remember? Say it in a creepy voice. Open your eyes wide. Jerk your head side to side."

She bugs her eyes and pivots her head, and moans, "'*P-a-a-a-a-a-a! We-e-e-e're a-a-a-all out-ta-a-a w-a-a-a-ter!*'"

It's about as scary as a soggy graham cracker, but I tremble and clutch her arm, then read Pa's line: "'Well, we should'"—I stop and check behind me—"'hit Rapid'"—I stop and look again—"'City a'fore . . . *sundown!*'" I shiver, then scream.

She jumps again, then laughs.

"I want you to scream," I say.

"What?" she whispers.

"Scream. You know. Like something terrifying just happened? Like, say, you failed a quiz?"

"I can't scream."

"Why not?"

"I just can't. Not in . . . here."

"You can't scream in your own room? Where can you—in the library?"

"My mom . . ."

"Scream, Eden. Scream your head off. Give me your best shot." This was what this whole exercise was about. I wanted to hear her really let go, to holler like Calamity Jane.

"Go on, do it," I say. "That's an order from your acting coach. Scream."

"Eeee!" she says, her straight white teeth showing.

I sigh loudly on purpose.

"That was pathetic."

"Oh," she says, and frowns.

"Try again, only this time try opening your mouth. Wide."

She tries. "Aaaaaa!"

"I'm not the dentist! Scream!"

"I *can't*, Zee." She starts nibbling her thumb. "I just can't."

There's a knock at the door. "Eden?" her mother says. "Are you okay? I'm hearing strange noises."

"It's okay, Mom!" Eden says, stiffening up. She's so tense, a sudden breeze could snap her in two. "We're fine. We're just rehears—"

I lunge at her suddenly and scream real snarly, like a leopard.

And she shrieks. It's loud, and piercing, and long. It's good.

Her mother frantically pushes open the door and rushes in. "Eden? Are you all right? What is it? What happened?"

"I . . . I told you," Eden says, gripping her heart. "We're acting."

She looks at me with a grin.

I give her a thumbs-up.

31. My Starring Role Ate My Homework Tutor

Today is Day Five, the day of our dress rehearsal. My costume is a frilly, poufy, lacy, pink, full-length dress and a very wide-brimmed sun hat with a big purple bow attached. Eden's is a buckskin outfit with fringe. She carries a pistol; I carry a parasol. I'm so jealous I could lock her in a closet till after the play closes. But I don't.

We spent Day Four rehearsing scenes, singing songs, learning our entrances and exits, our cues and marks (where we're supposed to stand when we're onstage). Josh says we're ready to do the whole show. During dress rehearsal, we can't stop if we mess up. We're supposed to treat it like the real thing.

So everyone's pretty jittery and fidgety, but Eden is the jitteriest and fidgetiest. I can barely stand to look at her. Her eyes are swollen and red, like she's been crying or not sleeping or both. Probably both. She's been nervous as a cat during our after-school rehearsals. Her teeth are actually chattering. The girl's a mess.

"I can't do it, Zee!" she cries into the sleeve of my frilly, poufy, lacy, pink, full-length dress. "You have to play Calam. You *have* to!"

I give her a hug. She sure is tiny. "It's normal to be freaked out. You know the lines. You know your cues. You look great. Now just get out there and do it."

She swipes her face with her fingers. "Can you tell I've been crying?"

"Yes," I say, and chase her away. Then I sashay in my enormous pink dress over to my place backstage.

The buckskin jumpsuit is too big on her. It would fit me better. I know her lines. I know her cues and marks. I bet we could convince Josh to let us swap roles. But that wouldn't be right. It's Josh's call.

"All right," Josh says, then pauses for silence. When he has it, he yells "*Action!*" and runs out onstage.

He's wearing a buckskin outfit, too, and a wig of long curly brown hair He's not wearing his glasses. He must have contacts. The first scene is all his.

"'Ladies and gentleman, my name is James Butler Hickok, but my friends call me Wild Bill. This ain't the tale of the legendary Wild Bill Hickok, though, as interestin' and deservin' of a delightful musical play as my life is. No, this here play is the tale of one Martha Jane Canary. You probably know her as Calamity Jane. We begin when she was jus' thirteen years old, crossin' the prairie in a covered wagon with her family. They'd left behind their home in Princeton, Missouri, and were headin' to Virginia City, Montana, over a thousand miles away, which is an awful long way when you're travelin' by stagecoach with a sick mama through treacherous territory.'"

This is the cue for the covered wagon to be pushed out. The actors playing the Canary family pretend to bump along in it.

"'Are we there yet, Ma?'" Lije Canary (Cooper) says.

"'You ast that question twelve million times, Lije Canary,'" young Martha (Eden) says. "'Cain't ya see Ma's feelin' poorly?'" And she faux-conks Cooper on the head.

Eden's not talking nearly loud enough, or sassy enough, and the conk looked more like a tag.

"'Ow!'" Cooper says, which is his line exactly as written.

When I get a chance, I grab Eden and tell her to speak up.

"I'll try," she mutters, but her mind seems far away.

She doesn't speak up. She stammers and flubs her lines, or forgets them. She drops her gun three times.

"You have to play Calam," Wain whispers to me. "She'll ruin the show."

I don't answer. At this point I don't care about the show. It's Eden I'm worried about. She's a wreck. I need to help her.

Hold on just a second! Did I, Zaritza May Dalrymple, just say that I didn't care about the *show*?

What in the world is happening to me?

32. My "Dog" Ate My Perfect Taco

We're supposed to be at the theater/cafeteria by six fifteen. My mother made an early dinner, and it's my favorite: tacos. The table is covered with small dishes and bowls filled with grated cheese, spicy beef, refried beans, salsa, sour cream, guacamole (yuck), and chopped lettuce. I take a taco shell and fill it with (the order is important): beans, meat, a ton of cheese, and a little lettuce on top. My mother goes vegan: no meat, no cheese, no sour cream. My father likes the works. Abby has a plastic bowl of beans and cheese.

"Spoon, Abby," Mother says, when Abby drops her face into the bowl.

"I'm worried about Eden," I say. "She's a wreck.

She was shaking so hard during dress rehearsal her teeth chattered."

"Too bad," Mother says. "She's such a nice girl." She bites into her taco, and it explodes. That's the problem with vegan tacos: they don't hold together. You need cheese for glue.

"She's *too* nice," I say. "She's terrified to let loose. I think it's her mother. She totally freaked out when I made Eden scream."

My mother gives me the hand-on-hip, chin-pulled-in look, like I did something wrong.

"What? We were *acting*."

"It sounds as if she let loose when you told her an Asian couldn't play Calamity Jane," Mother says, as she picks at her broken taco.

"Yeah, *that* was totally out of charac—"

Hey!

"Mother, you're a genius! She had no problem telling me off that day. And in front of everybody, too."

"Are you concocting some fiendish plot?" Father asks. He rubs his hands together. "Because if you are, count me in!"

"Stop it, Paul. Zaritza, you are not to say

offensive things to your friend in order to get her riled up enough to play a character in a play."

Sometimes she's so psychic it's scary.

"I was only kidding, of course," Father says sheepishly. "Now, no fiendish plots, Zaritza. If we've told you once, we've—"

"Are you listening to me, Zee?" Mother says, leaning toward me.

"Abby has her face in her food again," I say, which is classic subject-changing. Baby sisters are handy as distractions.

"Spoon, Abby!" Mother says, turning away from me. "Spoon! Spoon!"

"Poo!" Abby says, and waves it in the air.

I lean over and start a conversation with Father about his day while Mother mops up Abby's mess.

"I don't see why my students keep asking to sing their favorite pop songs in choir," Father says. "Are teenagers not into madrigals anymore?"

"I don't know. What's a madrigal?"

"I guess that's my answer."

Out of nowhere, Wormy pops up onto my lap, drags my taco off my plate, and then jumps to the floor, where he licks the meat and cheese out. He leaves the lettuce.

"Devil 'dog'!" I screech (with finger quotes).

He runs from the kitchen. I fly after him.

"Zee, we didn't finish our conversa—" I hear Mother call after me, but I pretend I can't hear.

"Dogs" can be great distractions, too.

33. My Homework Wrecked My Chance to Faux-Offend Her

It's dark out when we get to the school, which always feels creepy and exciting. Kids from my class are arriving with their families, too. I spot Wain and run over to him.

"Opening night!" he says, and puts up a hand for a high five.

I slap it. "Let's get inside. I've got a fiendish plot to save the show, but I don't have much time."

The theater/cafeteria looks more like a theater tonight. There are rows of chairs facing the stage, the first set is ready, and someone is tinkering with the stage lights. Hannah, probably. Aaron's mother is warming up on the piano. She's dressed in a long black dress with a white lace collar and is wearing black high heels. I've never seen her look so snazzy.

There's a table set up with a roll of tickets, a cashbox, and a stack of programs. Caitie and Tristan will sell tickets till showtime, then run backstage. Family members don't get in free, not even parents. When I make it big, I'll buy my parents all the tickets they want so they can see me in every one of my many, many performances. They may have to buy their own movie tickets, but I'll be sure they get to attend my premieres in Hollywood.

Wain and I leave our families in line and rush off to find Eden, but we don't see her anywhere. Neither has anyone else. I wonder if she faked a sore throat or something and stayed home. I don't want that to be true, but I can't say I'd be crushed.

"We should get in costume," Wain says.

"I'm going to wait for Eden."

"Just in case you're asked to put on buckskins?"

"No," I lie. He knows me too well. "I just want to be sure she's okay."

At six thirty the seats are half-filled and Eden

is still not here. I see Ms. Tsots schmoozing with parents, and some of the teachers hanging out together over by the wall, probably comparing notes on bad kids. I wonder if they are truly excited for the play, or if they feel put out having to work on a Friday night. At least Mr. O. had an easy week.

"Anyone seen Eden?" Josh calls out, concern in his voice.

"I haven't," I say.

After he's gone, I smile. I can't lose tonight. If Eden doesn't show up, I'll get to play Calam. If she does, I'll act upset and finally confess the "truth" I've been hiding: I'm angry that she stole my part; I've never seen worse acting than hers in my life; I don't really like her; and I only helped her because my mother made me. Oh, yeah— and that an Asian girl can't play Calamity Jane. I don't mean any of it, of course, but it will make her blow her top, and she will give the performance of a lifetime, and our play will be a smash success. Plus I will be credited with saving the show.

Either way, I win.

Josh passes by me again later. "Why aren't you in costume, Zaritza? Curtain's in fifteen!"

"It is?" I say, pretending I haven't been checking the cafeteria clock every ten seconds. "Don't worry. I'm an expert at getting into costume fast." And I snap my fingers.

This was my very clever way of letting Josh know that, if need be, I could get into *Eden's* costume at a moment's notice. Which is why I haven't gotten dressed yet. Why get into it if I'm just going to have to get out of it again? How hard can it be to slide a buckskin over your head and smudge your face with damp cocoa powder to make it look dirty?

It looks like that's just what I'm going to have to do. I can't see Eden being late like this without a reason. And she wasn't sick today. Not physically sick, anyway. She is emotionally sick. Afraid sick. She might be throwing up for all I know.

At six fifty I go into the girls' bathroom, which is our temporary dressing room, and start undressing . . . real . . . slow.

Then I hear someone say, "She's here! Eden's here!"

Eden bursts into the room, breathless, flustered, her eyes red and puffy.

"Hey, Eden!" I say with a big, faux smile. "Glad you ma—"

"Can't talk," she grunts. She grabs her buckskins off a hook and locks herself in a stall.

"Curtain is in—" I start to say, but she cuts me off. "Not *now*, Zee! *Leave me alone!*"

Hmm. Maybe I won't have to make her mad after all. She's plenty worked up already.

Before I finish getting into my costume, she busts out of the stall. She rushes over to the mirror and starts smudging on her makeup.

"Everything okay?" I ask.

"Perfect!" she shouts. "I made up one excuse after another, but *no-o-o-o-o*! My mother said I had a responsibility to do the play. So here I am!"

"Ooh, I hate the R-word," I say sympathetically.

"I hate *acting*!" she snarls.

This is good. I don't need to do a thing. Unless she cools off, of course. Then I'll have to insult her. As her acting coach and friend, it would be my duty.

34. My Homework Ate Up the Applause

Minutes later, the lights overhead flicker. The audience claps. It's showtime.

Josh and Hannah move through the backstage area making last-minute checks and shushing everyone. Hannah is dressed up tonight: a purple, sequined gown and black high heels. She leaves Josh behind and steps onstage, to a big round of applause.

"Hello and welcome, everyone, to tonight's performance of *Calamity Jane*. My name's Hannah and I'm one of the directors of tonight's show. Josh, the other director, will be out in a moment. You'll recognize him. He'll be the tallest actor in the play tonight."

Mild laughter. I wonder how many times

she's told that joke. Not enough to get the timing right . . .

She goes on to talk a little bit about the troupe and its mission, and reminds everyone to turn off their electronic devices, and not to take flash pictures, and *blah blahbity blah* while we are all going quietly crazy in the tiny, cramped back-stage area. At long last, she says, "And now, enjoy *Calamity Jane!*"

Josh rushes out and delivers his first speech and we have to wait some more till, finally, he says his cue—"treacherous territory"—and the stagehands push out the covered wagon. Eden, still freaked out of her mind, takes her place behind it.

Break a leg! I mouth at her.

"If only!" she whispers back.

Things look bad right off the bat, when she misses her first cue, but at least she remembers the line: "'You ast that question twelve million times, Lije Canary!'" She delivers it with a rea-sonable amount of sass, a lot more than usual.

The Canarys sing their song and the next scene starts and, in general, things are going pretty well. You have to keep in mind that the cast—minus Josh—is a bunch of inexperienced fifth graders who learned this whole play in five days. A lot of lines get mumbled, stuttered, or forgotten, and there's a fair amount of collisions as kids forget where they're supposed to go and how to get there. But Josh is out there, filling in lines and directing traffic. It's not Broadway, but it's not horrible, either.

Eden is surprisingly good. She's louder and feistier than she has been, mostly because she's furious, but probably also because this is the first time she's done the play—*any* play—in front of a real live audience. Standing up in front of people tends to make a person either freeze up or come to life. Her mother is out there, of course, which must make her crazy, but the lights are so bright, you can't make out any faces. Besides, I bet a part of her wants to show her mother what she can do. Then there's all that pent-up nervous energy you feel as you get closer and closer to showtime. It can make you want to jump right out of your skin. The funny thing is, though, is that as soon as you hit the stage, with the crowd and the lights, all that nervous energy turns into really good energy, the kind you need to be able to project your voice and be bigger than you are in real life. That doesn't happen in rehearsal. You have to be an experienced stage actor to know it.

Now Eden knows it.

As people clap and cheer at her jokes and songs, she gets better and better. I only get glimpses of her from backstage, but I can hear in her voice how relaxed she's getting. She's starting to enjoy herself, to find out how much fun being in a play is. I'm happy that she's feeling that. She sure worked hard and went on even though she was terrified. She deserves to feel it.

I see now why Josh picked her.

I'm just as proud of her as I can be. I am her acting coach, you know. Not that I want credit for it. I'm sure Eden will tell everyone afterward she owes it all to me. Who knows, maybe one day she'll win an Oscar or a Tony and when she's up there at the podium she'll thank me, her acting coach, who made it all possible.

"Zaritza!" Wain whispers.

I snap out of my daydream.

"That's your cue."

"Oh!" I say, and hustle my bustle onstage.

Before I hit my mark, I'm in character. Snooty. Refined, though not as refined as I think. I live in Deadwood, South Dakota, after all. A busybody who wants people to act civilized. I like the role. It's a stretch. Challenging. True, it's small, but I'm no small actor.

I join the other Deadwood Ladies (Jacqueline and Melodie, that is) to confront Calamity Jane. Then I hear a loud "Zuzza!" from the audience, followed by a wave of laughter. That's my little sister for you. Always trying to steal the show.

When the laughter dies down, Eden says to Lady #1, "'A body who ain't wearin' trousers had better stay inside where there ain't any rattlers, cuz in a frilly frock like yourn it's a lot easier to git bit!'" Then she tries to bite her. She really hisses and snaps like a rattler, too.

I roll my eyes up at the sky (a.k.a., the cafeteria ceiling) and twirl my parasol.

"'That's no excuse for dressing like a man,'" I say, then roll my eyes down at Eden/Calam, who's glaring at me with her chin stuck out. I can barely believe it's her, she looks so sassy and ornery. "'I've been wearing a dress for years,'" I say smugly, "'and I've never had any trouble with snakes.'"

The audience bursts into laughter. Oh, I love that! It feels *so good!*

"'Ya never rode bareback, neither, I bet,'" Eden/Calam says, then gives a snort.

"'Of course not!'" I say.

"'An' ya ain't ridden into battle, yer pistols blazin'?'"

"'Certainly not. I am a *lady*, ma'am.'"

"'Then ladies sure miss out on a heap a' excitement!'"

And she fires her gun into the air. Backstage, Aaron slams two boards together: *BANG!*

Though of course I know it's coming, I screech and go all to pieces. I clatter my hard heels on the floor and let my parasol fly. I wait for the huge laugh to simmer down, then deliver the punch line:

"'F-Firing g-guns is n-n-n-not what I c-c-call f-f-f-f-f-fun!'" Then, in baby talk, I add, "'It's dangewous and it huwts my dewicate eaws.'"

I bring my dainty white gloves up to them.

This gets a hugh laugh. Small role, big actor.

That's our cue to break into "Shootin' Off Your Mouth." I have a real good time singing my verse. Maybe that's because it's so opposite of who I am. It's fun to play against type. My verse goes like this:

I'm afraid, ma'am, we can't al-LOW-eth
Your shootin' guns off in the HOU-eth!
Oh, you might think we're high-BROW-eth,
Still, don't start shootin' off your MOU-eth!

After the song, we Ladies exit to a roar of applause. Jacqueline cuts the wrong way again (I don't think she knows her left from her right), but I anticipate it and avoid a collision. As I'm heading offstage I hear a whoop I recognize: it's Father's. It's okay that I don't hear my mother whoop. She's not really a whooper. I'm sure she's clapping and smiling.

There's not much play left after my scene. The whole cast goes onstage for the big finale, a reprise of "Who Doesn't Want to Be Brave?" At the end of the song we're all in a line at the front of the stage, our hands up in the air. We bow, then, on Josh's cue, we turn and rush offstage. The audience cheers behind us.

Josh sends us back out in the order we rehearsed, which is based on how big our roles were. I go out with the Ladies and bow, then take our places at center stage left. The Canary kids go out together, bow, and go to center stage right. Then Pa and Ma (Wain and Opal), Captain Caldwell (Sam), and Colonel Custer (Bianca). They bow and set up center stage.

Eden is last. She runs out to downstage center, and bows. The audience just roars. They stand up and clap and hoot and stomp their feet and wave their programs. It's insane. Eden stands there, herself again, embarrassed, blushing and covering her face with her hands, but shaking with uncontrollable laughter and squirting out giddy tears. I couldn't have been happier if it had been me. Really. No acting.

Hannah and Josh then step out onstage and they quiet everybody down for some announcements. They thank the school, and the teachers, and the parents, and Ms. Tsots, and *blahbity blah blah*. Then they remind everyone that there are two more performances tomorrow (*yay!*), a matinee and an evening show, and that preorders for video recordings of tonight's performance could be purchased in the lobby. Eden and I looked at each other and squeal. We could watch the play as many times as we wanted for the rest of our lives! *Woo-hoo!*

Then it's photo time, and parents come up and hand flowers to their kids. Mother hands me a single white rose, which is so elegant. Then we gather for group shots. *Flash, flash, flash, flash.* Josh makes it fun by calling out poses: "Monsters!" "Fairies!" "Gorillas!" "Lunatics!" When it's finally over, we run backstage to change.

I go looking for Eden, but I'm not alone. Everyone's crowding around her and telling her how amazing she was. But she breaks through and runs right to me. *Wham!* Big hug.

"You were brilliant!" I say. "I knew you would be. I just knew it!"

Not exactly the truth, I know, but it plays well. It's a good scene.

"I couldn't have done it without you," she sobbed, and squeezed harder.

"Yes, you could have. But thanks."

"Magnificent job, everybody!" Josh is saying as he comes over. "And you, Calamity *Eden*, I knew you had it in you. Sometimes it takes a packed house to bring it out."

Exactly what I thought! And I don't have the years of experience he has. Not bad, huh?

I do have to hand it to him, though. I thought he was nuts, but picking Eden for the lead was good casting. I mean, he should have picked *me*, but he didn't make the horrible mistake I thought he did.

"You killed them out there, Lady Number Three," he says to me. "You've got great comic chops, Ferret Girl. You had them eating out of your hand!"

"Thanks, Josh!" I gush, like I'm five or something. And I'm not acting. It was a really nice thing to say.

I run to get out of my costume and makeup so I can go tell my parents the nice thing Josh said.

35. My Homework Made Her Mother Cry

Eden's mother is standing with my family and Wain's when the three of us come out. I don't know where Eden's father is. She never talks about him, actually.

"Zuzza!" Abby says, and everybody laughs.

"Did you hear her from the stage?" my mother asks, her face looks worn out from smiling. Which is so great. She hasn't been smiling enough.

I take Abby from her. "Yes, I heard you, baby sister. Don't you know you're not supposed to yell out the actor's name during a performance? Huh?"

I tickle her ribs, and she giggles and wriggles. I'm making light of it, but, really—she shouldn't yell out.

My mother uses her empty arms to give Eden a big hug. "You were fabulous, Eden!"

Fabulous? I don't think I've ever heard that word come out of her mouth before.

"You were indeed!" Father adds. "You were a supreme delight. *Brava! Brava!*" And he gave a quick, crisp *clap-clap-clap.*

"How about me?" I say, acting a little hurt, but feeling ... well ... a little hurt. "Wasn't I fabulous? Wasn't I a supreme delight?"

"You were a fabulous, delightful *marvel*, my dear," Father says, and takes my face in his hands and kisses one cheek then the other. "A *brilliant* musical/comedian with *expert* timing. And inimitable panache. How's that?"

"Better," I say, though I'm not sure I understood that last part.

Wain's parents make a fuss about Eden, too, and me, and Wain, and my parents make a fuss about Wain, who really was excellent in his sturdy supporting role. In other words, it was a praisefest. A hugfest. Only one person held back, and it was like we all noticed it at the same time.

"You must be so proud of Eden," Wain's father says to Melissa. "She's acted before, yes?"

Wain doesn't keep his father in the loop much.

Eden walks over to her mother and leans against her, like she's trying to make this easier for her. Why is it so hard?

"No," Melissa says, and then chokes up a little. She tries to hide it by twisting Eden's hair with her fingers. "This is her first . . ." She chokes up again. Maybe there are too many people. I think of how difficult it is for Eden to speak in groups— when she's not mad at me, that is.

"I'm really proud . . ." she gets out, but then she has a major choke-up. She covers her face with her hands, and Eden squeezes her around the middle.

"It's okay, Mom," she says softly.

"What do you say, everyone—ice cream?" Father says, coming to Melissa's rescue. "When I was a kid I loved the stuff. Do kids still like ice cream, Wain?"

"We do!" Wain answers.

Melissa smiles, and a tear streaks down her

face. She swipes it away with her finger and says, "That would be nice."

It's raw. It's real. I must store it away for later use.

36. My Homework Sang Me to Sleep

It's after midnight. I can't sleep. Bandito's burrowed under my pillow, making his chattery night noises, but that's not what's keeping me awake. I've gotten used to them. I like them, in fact. The room felt too quiet all week when he wasn't here. I'm used to his stink, too, as crazy as that sounds. No, what's keeping me awake is trying to think of a way for me to keep the mustelid for good.

How's that for a surprise twist? Girl meets ferret. Girl hates ferret. Ferret does weasel war dance. Girl loves ferret. Girl does weasel war dance.

Mr. O. was sure surprised when I asked him after the matinee if I could take Bandito home for the rest of the weekend.

"But you don't have any homework to make up," he said.

"You said extra credit was only for kids who were all caught up," I answered. "That's why I want Bandito. To store up some extra credit, just in case . . ."

He bought it, even though it wasn't the real reason. But I think he knows that I secretly like Bandito.

I climb out of bed and click on the lamp on my dresser and look into the mirror. I still have a little makeup on my eyelids from tonight's performance. Our final performance, sadly. I hate it when a show's run ends.

I make my face droopy and ashamed. "Bandito escaped, Mr. O. I left the cage door open. I'm terribly sorry. I know he was my responsibility and, believe me, I take my responsibilities very seriously. Just ask my mother. She has taught me the importance of—"

I pretend to break down here. Then I take a deep, long breath.

"No, I can't lie. It wasn't me. It was my . . . . . . sister who opened the door."

No. Erase. I can't blame the baby. That would be unjust.

"My father loves Bandito, you see, and after a hard day at work—my father's a public school teacher, too—he likes to take Bandito out of his cage and . . ."

Again no. I have to face it. If I'm going to pretend Bandito escaped so that I can keep him forever, I'm going to have to take the blame myself, and face the punishment alone.

"Mr. O., it was I who left the cage open. It is all my fault, and I will do whatever is required to make it up to you. If you want, I'll replace him—"

Wait. How much does a ferret cost? It doesn't really matter, because I'm broke. I spent my last five dollars on stroopwafels.

And I can't exactly keep Bandito *and* ask my mother for money to replace him, can I? I haven't even figured out how I'm going to convince her to let me keep him. But I have to keep him. I love him.

"You see, Mother, everyone at school keeps complaining about how bad the smell is. The kids. The teachers. The parents. Even the principal. No one can think or study or anything with him in the classroom. So Mr. O. said he was going to take him to the animal shelter and have him put down, and, of course, I said, 'No! You mustn't! I'll bring the poor, defenseless, creature home . . .'"

No. Mother would check with Mr. O. Besides, she hates the smell, too.

"Guess what, Mother? The health department said we had to get rid of Bandito! He has—"

No. If the health department said no, so would Mother.

"Bandito's gotten really skinny, Mother. He won't eat. Mr. O. said he wasn't adapting very well to his surroundings in the classroom, so I said maybe we could adopt him."

Hmm. Not bad. *Not adapting to his surroundings* sounds like a phrase Mr. O. would say. It's probably where I heard it.

But wait. Erase. Same problem as before. Mother would check with him first. Why do adults have to do that? Go over kids' heads, I mean.

All of a sudden Bandito pops out from under my pillow and starts *dook-dook-dook*-ing.

"What's wrong, Bandy?" That's what I call him now.

"Zee?" my mother asks.

I shriek. Mother is standing there in her old purple robe, her eyes barely open, her hair a disaster. She clicks on the light.

"You have to stop sneaking up on me like that or you are really going to give me a heart attack!"

"What are you doing up so late?" she asks in a croaky voice.

"I couldn't sleep."

"Because of Bandito's chattering?"

"No. I'm used to that. In fact, I like his noises. And his smell."

I put out my hand, and he runs up my arm to my shoulder and nuzzles my neck, like he does to Father.

"Are you still wound up because of the play?"

"No. I'm wound down."

"You were so good tonight," she says.

"You didn't like the matinee?"

"You were so good in the matinee, too."

"Thanks. Eden was terrific, huh?"

"Yes, she was. And you were terrific for helping her. You're a good friend."

"Can we keep this from getting corny?"

"Sorry. So you want a ferret?"

I look up at her. "You heard that?"

"I doubt you can keep your class's pet, but you could ask Mr. O., see what he says. . . ."

"What if he says no?"

She shrugs. "We could maybe look for another one?"

I push myself away from her. *"Really?* You'd get me one?"

"Maybe. But, really, Zee, you don't have to make up these elaborate schemes to get what you want, or to get out of what you've done." She tilts her head and gives me a knowing look. "Just be honest."

"I want Bandito," I say.

"It would make things pretty crowded around here."

"Why don't we get rid of Wormy? Eden likes him— "

"Wormy stays. He's our—"

"No R-word, please."

"Sorry. But if we get a ferret, it would be your . . . R-word."

"That's fine! So can we get one?"

"Maybe. There's something you need to know first."

"Whether Mr. O. will let me have Bandito? I'll ask him on Monday."

"No, not that." She pauses. Dramatically. " . . . . . . You're going to have a brother."

"What? You're not talking about the ferret, now, are you? Because that's weird if you are . . ."

"No, I mean a brother. A human brother. I'm three months pregnant."

"Really?" I lay my hand on her belly through her purple robe. Pregnant? I wonder if that's what has been making her so crabby. "There's a baby in there? You're not very fat."

"Thanks."

"Who's going to stay home and take care of this one? Me?"

"I'm due in June during summer vacation. I'll stay home for a while, but then I'll be going back to work. Your father will take care of the baby, but he'll need your help. He'll have a lot on his plate. The baby, Abalina, Wormy . . . you."

"And Bandy. Hopefully."

At this moment, he's down the back of my outside pajama top. I wear two when he sleeps with me so he doesn't scratch my skin. He likes slinking around between them.

"Only if you promise to help out around here. To be . . . R-word."

I think this over.

"If I help Father with the brother and the sister and the pets, can I get my ears pierced? Maybe for my birthday?" Which is August sixteenth.

"I'll tell you what. Start wearing your glasses every day, and you can get your earrings now."

She grins at me like she knows I didn't lose them. Did she find where I hid them? That's impossible. Unless maybe Wormy dug them up. . . .

"Deal," I say, and stick out my hand to shake on it. As she takes it I add, "But I get contacts as soon as possible, right? An actor can't wear glasses."

"We'll talk about it later," she says. "Now, let's

get some sleep. Wain and Eden and their families are coming over for brunch in the morning."

"Yeah! We're going to do some improv. You said we could record it on your phone, remember?"

She nods as she nudges me toward my bed, then sits beside me after I slip under the covers. Bandy dives down between the sheets to my feet.

Mother strokes my hair real gently, which gives me the chills. It always does. The sleeve of her purple robe tickles my nose. Her robe really smells like her. In fact, I think it smells more like her than she does.

"You're still my little girl, you know," she says, and her eyes get all misty.

"No, Mother, *Abby* is your little girl. I'm the big one."

"You'll always be my little girl."

"Cor. Ny."

"You're right. You are big. Acting onstage in front of a whole room of people. I could never do that. You were so good tonight."

"You already said that," I mumble. I'm starting to drift off.

213

She kisses my forehead and stands up.

"Good night, Mother," I say, yawning.

"Good night, Zee," she says, and clicks off the light.

Bandy slithers back in between my pajama tops.

"Good night, fur," I say.

I fall asleep listening to him chatter.